AF417114

The Best Erotic Short Stories of 2023 2-Volumes-In-1

Explicit Adult Erotica Featuring First Times, Threesomes, Anal Sex, Roleplay, Gang Bangs, Lesbian Sex, Cuckold, Older-Younger, Taboo, and more...

Rayna Russell

© **Copyright GO Publishing LLC 2024 - All rights reserved.**

The content contained within this book may not be reproduced, duplicated or transmitted without direct written permission from the author or the publisher.

Under no circumstances will any blame or legal responsibility be held against the publisher, or author, for any damages, reparation, or monetary loss due to the information contained within this book. Either directly or indirectly. You are responsible for your own choices, actions, and results.

Legal Notice:

This book is copyright protected. This book is only for personal use. You cannot amend, distribute, sell, use, quote or paraphrase any part, or the content within this book, without the consent of the author or publisher.

Disclaimer Notice:

Please note the information contained within this document is for educational and entertainment purposes only. All effort has been executed to present accurate, up-to-date, and reliable, complete information. No warranties of any kind are declared or implied. Readers acknowledge that the author is not engaging in the rendering of legal, financial, medical or professional advice. The content within this book has been derived from various sources. Please consult a licensed professional before attempting any techniques outlined in this book.

By reading this document, the reader agrees that under no

circumstances is the author responsible for any losses, direct or indirect, which are incurred as a result of the use of the information contained within this document, including, but not limited to, — errors, omissions, or inaccuracies.

Contents

Introduction, Volume 1 — 7

1. Long Time Cumming — 9
By Nia Long

2. Dear Diary — 27
Moran Fitzpatrick

3. Watermelon — 43
Chrissy Lowell

4. Wild Ella — 59
By Clifford Brannum

5. Christine's First Gangbang — 75
By Richard Kinney

6. The Massage — 91
By Marine Leland

7. He Likes To Watch — 107
By Victoria Jimenez

8. Mistress — 121
My Amanda Moss

9. Who's The Boss — 137
By Jordan W. Miller

10. Sorry, Daddy — 153
By Lisa Wilton-James

Afterword — 169

Introduction, Volume 2 — 171

11. Renée's First Time — 173
by Renée Archer

12. Her Recruits — 189
by Chantal Marshall-Sisk

13. Beth Day Ever
by Stuart Goldman 205

14. Happy Anniversary
by Eva Cortez 221

15. Dove's Porn Fantasy
by Jena Costello 237

16. She's Been Waiting For You
by Charlotte P. Grace 251

17. The BBQ
By Clay Roth 267

18. Whatever You Want, Sir
By Joe Parks 283

19. Jade
by Stefanie Jones 299

20. Dear Cara
by Phillip Andres 313

Afterword 329

Introduction, Volume 1

Hello friends!!!

This is your friendly purveyor of smut, Rayna. I'm so glad to be back with another anthology of the best erotic stories of the year. I received so much generous feedback from last year's anthology, and I've integrated a lot of your thoughts into this new volume. Most notably, I sought out some more writers of color to bring some new, sexy perspectives. If you're listening to the audiobook version, I've also brought in some fantastic new voices to bring these short stories to life!

For those of you who are new - welcome! I'm a writer and editor and a voracious reader of erotic fiction.

My favorite format for erotica, by far, is short stories. The writer is challenged to bring a plot to life in a few minutes, which really creates fast, fun plots. And you can sample different kinds of stories without much commitment. You may discover some things you didn't even know turned you on.

This book has everything, from sweet first-time stories to the raunchiest gang bangs. And each writer brings a unique voice. I'm personally absolutely in love with this collection, and I hope you are too.

And feedback is always welcome! Send me a message at RaynaRussellErotica@gmail.com

Are you a writer? Submit a story for consideration in a future volume! I find that 3000 words is the perfect length.

Relax and enjoy The Best Erotic Short Stories of 2023... Volume 1!

XOXO,
   Rayna

Long Time Cumming
By Nia Long

"How in the world did I get here?" Bria murmured as she shook her head, staring at the wall across from her in disbelief.

Nathan paused, pulling his lips away from her neck, where he'd been leaving a trail of sloppy kisses. He frowned as he leaned back to look at her. "Are you really that drunk? You don't remember us getting locked in here fifteen minutes ago? I guess you really are a lightweight. I only saw you drink like two beers."

"Shut up." Bria scowled. "I'm not that drunk—" Although her head was spinning and her words were slurred and, yeah, she was a lightweight. This was only her second college party, after all, and she'd never drunk at parties before. She'd refused to have a single sip of an alcoholic beverage before she turned 21, unlike most of her friends. "I wasn't asking literally—" How could she possibly forget how they'd ended up here? It had been borderline traumatic!

It had all started when Bria had decided to sit with a group of her best friend's friends, who Bria didn't know well or happen to like all that much. She found them all obnoxious, and she wasn't a fan of anyone who willingly chose to spend their time hanging around Nathan, who she'd known—and hated with every fiber in her being—since kindergarten. And wouldn't you know it, at the very center of the big group of assholes was Nathan, who they all seemed to adore.

Bria had been hesitant to join them the moment she saw Nathan sitting with them, but her options had been limited. It was either stick with her best friend, one of the only people she happened to know at this party, and hang out with the jolly group of assholes, or wander off to make some friends of her own. Naturally, she'd chosen the former option.

But that resulted in her being put on the spot about an hour later when the rowdy group started discussing their sex lives and eventually prying into hers, and her drunken, blabber-mouthed best friend had revealed that Bria had never fucked anyone in her life, which only resulted in everyone that had been around to hear it oohing and ahhing and teasing her until she just wanted to evaporate on the spot.

And Bria got the surprise of a lifetime when Nathan—who had made it his business to tease, insult, and spite her every chance he got since they were still in pull-ups—jumped to her defense.

Long story short, that had only resulted in the group collectively deciding to tease him too, and somehow, the two of them had been hauled off and locked in a closet together soon after. It was all a blur, really, and Bria wasn't even trying to remember it.

The embarrassment was too much for her to bear, and this was definitely going to be added to the list of memories that she kept locked away in a box long-forgotten in the back of her mind.

"Well then, how were you asking?" Nathan slurred, tilting his head.

"What?" Bria blinked.

"If you weren't asking literally, then how were you asking?"

"...Metaphorically? I don't know," Bria sighed, slumping back against the wall and twirling one of her thin braids around her fingers as her doe eyes traveled up toward the ceiling. "I just mean...How did I end up in a closet, at a party, with my worst enemy about to take my virginity? That's…I can't even comprehend how I ended up in this predicament. I mean—I hate you, you know!" She pointed a stern finger at him, and he merely raised his brows.

"Yeah, you've mentioned it." A thousand times, probably. "I'm not your biggest fan either, sweetheart, but even annoying little know-it-all goody-two-shoes who need to be knocked off their high horses like you can be pretty hot sometimes, so I'm not gonna complain about being trapped with you if it means I get to fuck you. Which…It would be nice if we could get to that part anytime soon, by the way. Don't you think we've done enough talking for tonight?"

"You're such a fucking pig," Bria huffed. "And I resent that. I'm not an annoying, know-it-all, goody-two-shoes who needs to be—"

"Yeah, yeah." Nathan waved her off, rolling his eyes as he ran a hand through his ginger hair. "I'm just saying, I can't imagine a sweet little virgin girl like you is gonna be able to rush into anything. We'll probably have to take it slow, so if you want to pop your cherry tonight, we're gonna need to move things along before someone remembers we're in here and comes to get us."

What Nathan said made sense, but Bria still squinted her eyes at him. "Don't say it like that. Just because I haven't fucked half the city like you have doesn't mean—"

"Why do you always have to argue with me?" Nathan grumbled as he massaged his temples.

"Because you're always wrong about everything," Bria stated matter-of-factly.

"Do you always behave like a twelve-year-old child when you get drunk?"

"I'm not behaving like a twelve-year-old child, you are!"

"You're such a fucking brat," Nathan growled. "This is why I can't stand you!"

"You weren't complaining about me being a brat when you offered to fuck me," Bria scoffed.

"Right, because I figured you wouldn't be able to talk much while you were busy hanging off my cock," he snapped.

"That's assuming your dick is any good," Bria muttered. "You talk so much shit and yet you probably don't even know how to fuck a woman the right way. Out of the hundreds of thousands of girls that you've been with, how many have you actually managed to make cum?" She rolled her eyes.

Nathan growled, and Bria gasped as he suddenly

grabbed hold of her legs, yanking on them until she'd slid down the wall and onto her back. He pushed her skirt up until it was bunched up around her waist and began tugging her panties down, biting his lip as he stared at the hot-pink, lace fabric. It contrasted perfectly with her chocolate skin, and there was a dark spot right in the center of them which made Nathan smirk.

"Guess the sweet little virgin girl is pretty turned on by the thought of being fucked by her 'worst enemy' inside the closet at someone's party. How cute."

"Don't give yourself too much credit," Bria grumbled, her cheeks burning as she quickly held a hand out to stop him from pulling her panties down. "I'm just—I've just been..." Really, what was she supposed to say to defend herself here?

If she was going to be honest, she was turned on by the situation at hand. As much as she couldn't stand Nathan, she had to admit that she'd always found him attractive. His pale skin, red hair, and piercing green eyes...His sharp jawline, deep voice, and lean yet muscular body...

The way he tended to look at her as if he wanted to rip her clothes off at any given moment...

She'd told him that she just wanted to lose her

virginity and didn't give a damn who took it, even if it had to be him of all people, and that was true, but also, maybe she wasn't as nonchalant as she'd made herself out to be. If she'd been stuck in here with anyone else, she never would have agreed to let them fuck her. But Nathan was someone that she'd known for a long time and trusted, in some strange way, despite his tendency to behave like a humongous asshole on most occasions. Plus, he looked like a model. So there was that.

"What, are you always this wet?" Nathan raised a brow. "In a permanent state of arousal just like a bitch in heat...I'm not surprised. I always thought you were secretly a slut." He smirked.

"I am not—stop that!" She smacked his hand away when he attempted to tug her panties down again, staring at him with wide eyes as he sent her a questioning look.

"I know this is your first time, but even you have to know that you've got to take your panties off if you want to get fucked."

Bria let out a deep breath, resting the palms of her hands against her cheeks to try to cool them down. "I know it's just—I've never...Well, you already know that," she muttered to herself.

Nathan let out a chuckle that sounded more like

a breath, his gaze softening as he stared at the shy-looking girl. "You know we don't have to do anything if you don't want to. It's fine if you've changed your mind."

"Yeah, right," Bria scoffed. "As if you wouldn't tease me about it for the rest of eternity if I decided to chicken out."

"I wouldn't." Nathan frowned. "Really, there are plenty of other things for me to make fun of you for. It's not like I need any new material anyway. If you don't feel comfortable, we don't need to do anything."

A small smile appeared on Bria's face as she stared at him for a few moments. The longer she looked into his honest eyes, the more she felt her anxiety starting to dissipate.

She made a conscious effort to loosen up, moving her hands away. "Go ahead."

"Are you sure?"

"Shouldn't we be moving things along before someone remembers we're in here and comes to find us?" she taunted, grinning when he rolled his eyes at her.

Nathan carefully pulled Bria's panties down, staring into her eyes the whole time and watching her expression closely. She seemed nervous, but that was to be expected, and at least now that she didn't look afraid.

When he was sure that she was okay with it, he pulled the panties all the way off and tossed them to the side, his eyes trailing down to stare at her cunt as he did. He licked his lips, his cock throbbing in his jeans as he pushed her thighs apart and repositioned himself so that he was lying between her legs.

"What are you—"

"I just wanna loosen you up a bit before I go trying to put my enormous cock inside you," Nathan chuckled. "Just relax and enjoy."

"Okay, well anyone who has to label their own cock as 'enormous' probably does not have an enormous cock, so maybe—" Bria cut herself off with a gasp, shooting up to rest her weight on her elbows as Nathan leaned down, immediately sticking his tongue out to get a taste of her.

He groaned as he pushed his tongue between her folds, flattening it as he licked a long strip up her center and then swirled it around her clit before allowing it to travel back down again.

Bria was already trembling, her thighs squeezing the sides of his head tightly as she stared at him with wide eyes. "Wow, okay—ugh, that feels really good!" she gasped, and Nathan chuckled, enjoying the way she squirmed and jolted every time he wriggled his tongue inside her hole or sucked on the lips of her cunt.

It didn't take long for Bria to start moving, grinding against his tongue and letting out quiet moans as she closed her eyes and focused on the foreign feeling. She pushed her top up, squeezing her breasts and arching her back, her moans growing louder as Nathan wrapped his arms around her thighs to hold her in place as he ate her with more vigor.

He spat on her hole, glancing up at her as he moved a hand down, rubbing his thumb over her clit before allowing it to trail down and push at her entrance.

Bria was too lost in her pleasure to be concerned with the fact that she was about to be penetrated by someone else's fingers for the very first time in her life, which was great. Nathan poked the tip of his thumb inside, then switched fingers, slowly pushing his pointer finger inside of her, then his middle finger and scissoring them to stretch her out.

Bria gasped when Nathan's fingers brushed up against her G-spot briefly before dipping back out of her again, and she could hardly stop twitching as he continued pushing his fingers in and out of her, soon adding a third just as he gave the inside of her thigh a sharp nip that caused her to hiss.

"Getting a bit loud there, aren't you?" he commented, wearing a sly grin, and Bria tried not to show her embarrassment as she realized that he was right. She hadn't even been attempting to hold her moans back, and maybe she should have, considering just how smug Nathan looked now.

"I..." Bria was yet again at a loss for words, unable to come up with an excuse quickly enough to keep his ego from blowing up even bigger than it already was.

"Trust me, baby, I don't mind. Just don't embarrass yourself by being so loud that people can hear you even over the music."

"You're such a fucking nuisance, Nathan, I swear —what are you doing?" Bria questioned quickly as Nathan moved away to push his pants down.

"Taking my dick out," he stated simply. "Assuming you still want it...You do still want it, right?"

"Yeah!" Bria nodded quickly before clearing her throat and shrugging her shoulders. "I mean—Yeah," she murmured, trying to appear nonchalant.

Nathan rolled his eyes, an amused smile playing on his lips as he pulled his cock out and gave himself a couple of strokes. Bria's mouth fell open as she stared at it, but she quickly schooled her expression into something far less impressed as he looked at her.

"That's..." *a big dick*, she wanted to say, but she wasn't going to give him that satisfaction. "A dick," she settled for saying instead.

"Wow, look who took sex ed back in middle school," he gasped before pushing her to lie flat on her back again. He hovered over her, leaning down until his face was only inches away from hers, and Bria's eyes flickered between his and his lips as his breath fanned over her face. "Are you ready?" His usual taunting voice was replaced by a much gentler one as he stared at her seriously, waiting patiently for her response.

"Yes." She nodded before swallowing around the lump in her throat. "Just...Go slow, okay?"

"Of course," he murmured, hesitating for only a moment before leaning down to press a kiss against her lips. The kiss was gentle, their lips just barely touching, mouths just barely moving against each other.

Bria melted into it easily, wrapping her arms around his neck and pulling him even closer as she tilted her head to the side, letting out a soft whine as he poked his tongue inside of her mouth.

The kiss heated up rapidly, the two of their mouths moving together in perfect sync as they devoured each other hungrily, tongues tangling and teeth clanking together as their hands began to roam each other's bodies.

Bria ran her hands along Nathan's broad shoulders and muscular back as Nathan's large hand gripped her side, his fingers rubbing over her hip before clutching her thigh and then traveling back up her stomach to grab her breast.

Bria hardly registered the tip of Nathan's cock breaching her as she was overwhelmed by his roaming hand and his tongue as it explored her mouth, but she gasped, letting out a choked moan when she felt his length slipping farther inside.

The stretch stung for a couple of seconds, and she hissed, tensing up as she pulled away from their kiss, but Nathan quickly shushed her before moving his hand up to stroke her cheek.

"It's okay, I'm not gonna move yet," he whispered. "Just focus on me."

When Bria gave him a slight nod, Nathan leaned forward, taking her mouth in for another kiss, this one rougher than the last.

Maybe he had been waiting to do this for a little while. Every time she pissed him off—which just so happened to be every time he spoke to her—maybe he fantasized about kissing her to shut her up and then fucking her into oblivion after. Maybe.

Nathan hissed as Bria clenched around him and squirmed until he quickly grabbed her hip to stop her. "Don't," he gritted out, and Bria pulled away from their kiss, breathless and grinning.

"What? What's wrong?" She clenched again, and Nathan squeezed his eyes shut, trying not to pay attention to the way his cock throbbed and twitched inside her. The way his stomach tensed up as pleasure coiled up in the pit of it, much faster than it usually did. He couldn't remember the last time he'd felt this needy.

"Don't be a fucking tease," he growled.

"Or what?" she questioned, trying to squirm around again.

Nathan stared at her for a few moments before pulling back and thrusting forward again slowly. Bria bit her lip, trying not to react, and Nathan smirked as he realized that she was more than ready for the long overdue pounding that he'd always wanted to give her.

"You'll regret being such a bitch to me," he grumbled.

Bria opened her mouth to say something smart,

but the words died on her tongue as Nathan wrapped his arms around her thighs again, pushing her knees up toward her head before he began fucking her with no mercy. Bria's breath was just about knocked out of her as Nathan started up a quick pace, slamming into her with all the speed of a jackhammer as he held her firmly in place. She was practically bent in half as he leaned down to kiss her again, but the kiss was brief as he pulled away to look at her. He wanted to see her while he fucked her. He wanted to watch the way her face contorted in pleasure, her mouth falling open and eyebrows furrowing together as she moaned uncontrollably, even as she attempted to keep herself quiet.

Bria wrapped her arms around the backs of her thighs to hold her legs up, tears filling her eyes and blurring her vision as she tried to keep staring into Nathan's. It just felt so good—better than she ever could have imagined, and the pleasure was already overwhelming. The way she felt so full with his cock buried deep inside of her, the way he fucked her open and pounded directly into her G-spot with every thrust, the way he muttered filthy words in her ear as he pushed his fingers into her mouth, forcing her to suck on them...

"That's it." He smirked. "Good fucking girl. See?

I knew I'd like you better like this. On your back for me, with your little pussy being split open on my cock and your mouth too busy for you to say anything obnoxious. Even the brattiest of fucking brats can be tolerable, just as long as they're kept busy enough. Maybe I should fuck you like this all the time. I bet we'd get along better."

Bria gurgled and moaned around his fingers, and that was about as much of a response as she could give him as her eyes rolled into the back of her head before slipping shut. Nathan could tell by the way her pussy was spasming that she was close, and he was too after having to wait so long to have her.

He pulled his fingers out of her mouth, grabbing her jaw and shaking her head around until she opened her eyes again. "You look at me. Look me right in the eyes while you cum on my cock."

"Nathan," Bria whimpered. "Oh my God, I—oh my f-fuck, shit—"

"I thought you said I didn't know how to fuck a woman right?" Nathan taunted. "Doesn't seem like you feel the same way now. Say it. Say you love the way I fuck you."

"I—I love the way you—" Bria gasped, shuddering as he pushed both of her legs to one side of him. The new position was somehow a thousand times better, and Bria shook her head, tears slipping down her cheeks as she pressed her hand against his stomach. "I'm—it's too much, I'm gonna cum—"

"Not a second before you tell me how much you love the way I fuck you. Say it."

"I love it, I-I love the way you—I love the way you fuck me, please—"

"Go ahead." Nathan grinned. "And remember the way it felt to cum all over my cock the next time you decide to mouth off to me."

Bria wasn't listening, already several galaxies away as she convulsed underneath him, moaning and muttering about how 'fucking good' he was, amongst other slurred curses and nonsensical phrases.

Nathan held out for as long as he could, fucking her through her orgasm until she could do nothing more than tremble beneath him and let out the occasional, shaky moan, but when he was sure that she'd come down from her high, he quickly pulled out of her and began stroking himself, groaning and throwing his head back as he came all over her stomach.

He was aware that he probably looked like a maniac as he laughed in between groaning, smirking lazily down at the worn-out girl as he stared at her prettily painted stomach, but he didn't care.

"Been waiting to do that for a while," he stated cheekily, chest heaving as he attempted to catch his breath after the last of his seed had spilled over her stomach.

"Me too," she hesitantly admitted. "Glad...glad I lost my virginity to you. I guess."

"Yeah, any girl would be."

"Shut the fuck up."

Dear Diary
Moran Fitzpatrick

Dear Diary,

You wouldn't believe the night I had!

And to think I'd been agonizing over the decision.

Do you remember how I told you that I had to choose between Tom and Ricky? Dating the two of them for the past few months has been amazing. I don't understand why they each had to go and ruin it by demanding that I choose.

As if I could possibly decide between the two....

Anyway, I'm glad that they pushed me to make a decision because I have had the best night of my life.

I want to write it all down so I can savor every exquisite detail.

Let me start at the beginning.

I'd been nervous as I sat across the table from Ricky. Up until a few moments earlier, he'd been sipping quietly on his drink, smiling over at me every so often. His green eyes had been alive and filled with humor when he arrived. He'd even stopped to rub my shoulders and give me a sweet kiss.

Soft music had been wafting from the speakers, punctuated by the occasional rise and fall of conversation. When the knots in my stomach had become too much for me to handle, I'd leaned back against the red vinyl booth and glanced around. With only a few people around us, the café had been largely quiet. Now and again, the group that had been sitting in the back laughed loudly, drawing our attention to them. Out of the corner of my eye, I'd noticed them glancing over at us, so I'd tossed my blond hair over my shoulders and straightened my back.

I'd known what they were thinking without asking.

Most of the time, whenever Ricky and I went out, we ended up getting the same confused looks, especially when we both stood up. Given that I was taller than Ricky and a lot louder, I'd grown used to being met with surprise.

Hell, I'd never even cared.

But I knew Ricky did.

So I'd let my eyes skim over the wooden tables lined up on either side of the cream-colored walls and paused at the tables scattered in the middle. Then I swung my gaze back to Ricky and lifted my lips into a slow, sensual smile.

"So what do you think?"

Ricky had cleared his throat and glanced down at his drink. "I don't know about this. This is a pretty big ask, Cal."

I'd shrugged and leaned forward against the table, offering him an obstructed view of my cleavage. In my knee-length yellow summer dress and tanned skin, I'd known that I had to use every tool at my disposal, including disarming Ricky with a dress that hugged my body in all the right ways.

He'd reacted the way I expected him to.

Even then, he hadn't been able to stop staring at me, a myriad of emotions dancing across his face. Unfortunately, I'd known from the second I walked in that it wasn't going to be easy. Getting Ricky to do what I wanted was one thing. Convincing him to engage in a threesome just so I could decide which man was a better fit was another.

And I'd had no way of knowing if either of them was going to say yes.

Considering Ricky's kind and docile nature, I'd known he'd be easier to win over. Having met him while I was picking up a shift at the bowling rink, the two of us had immediately hit it off. By the end of the night, he'd been all but ignoring his team and kept his eyes fixed solely on me.

It had been an intoxicating feeling.

You know the kind, diary.

As if I was drunk.

Last night hadn't been any different.

Ricky has a way of looking at me and making me feel like nothing else. Whenever he looked at me, it was like the world stopped turning, and I had to remind myself how to breathe. In spite of his serious and quiet nature, I knew what kind of man lurked underneath.

A thrill had raced through me at the thought of unleashing the beast within.

So much so that I'd continued to lean over the table until I took both of his hands in mine. He'd made a startled noise, but his eyes stayed on my face. I'd seen how much effort it took for him to hold completely still and refuse to answer my question altogether.

But I'd been determined to get my way.

A short while later, I'd stood up and wandered over to his side of the booth. As soon as I sat down, I'd placed a finger on his thigh and traced a path up. He'd sucked in a harsh breath when I'd leaned forward and palmed him.

"What are you doing?"

"Trying to make a case for myself," I'd replied breathlessly. "How am I doing so far?"

Ricky had struggled to swallow past the lump in his throat. "You do make a compelling case."

My fingers had given him another squeeze when he gasped, earning the attention of a uniformed waiter next to us. Ricky had offered him a tight, polite smile and turned his attention to the front. Quietly, he'd reached for his glass of water and downed it all in one gulp.

When he had finished his water, he reached for his soda.

Still, it hadn't deterred me.

On the contrary, it had made me want him even more.

He'd circled his fingers around my wrist and tugged. "I don't think is a good place for this."

I'd pouted. "But I want you."

Ricky had blown out a breath. "I want you too, but I'm not going to share you with anyone else."

"It's not sharing. Not in the long-term. It's just for a night."

Ricky had exhaled and linked his fingers together. "I just don't know if I'm comfortable with this arrangement. Why do you need this to prove something?"

I'd sighed and sat up straighter. "Because you're both amazing, and I want to have fun with both of you. There's no law that says I can't."

"No one said anything about a law."

I'd huffed, sat back, and crossed my arms over my chest. "So that's it?"

Ricky's expression had turned alarmed. "Now hang on a second—"

Before he'd finished his sentence, I'd been out of my seat, beaming. Tom Monroe had walked into the café and given me a mischievous grin before sweeping me into his arms. Once he'd set me down, I'd given him the once-over, starting with his ripped jeans, the shirt with paint splatters on it, and stopping at the shoulder-length brown hair falling in loose waves around his waves.

Tom had been looking especially hot.

I'd even considered dragging him off to the bath-room in the back, but I didn't want to leave Rick behind.

I'm stupid, aren't I, diary?

But then Tom's eyes had been studying me the entire time, bright blue and smoldering. "You look gorgeous."

And I'd melted into a puddle.

Have I mentioned how hot Tom is?

I'd beamed. "Thank you."

Suddenly, Tom had glanced over my shoulders at Ricky, who'd pressed his mouth into a thin white line. "What's up, Richard?"

"It's Ricky," he'd stressed with a lift of his chin. "What are you doing here?"

Tom had shrugged and thrown an arm over my shoulders. "Lie invited me."

"Lie," Ricky grumbled, underneath his breath. "I don't even know why."

"I invited him because this is about both of you," I'd said loudly. "I know you two don't like each other, but since I am seeing both of you, and you both want me to pick, I thought we should all talk about this like sane, mature people."

Ricky had snorted and sunk lower into his seat.

Then I'd removed Tom's arm from around my

shoulders and motioned from him to sit. He'd slid into the booth opposite Ricky and motioned to the waiter. Moments later, he'd given me a bright grin, making the butterflies in my stomach erupt.

Tom had his own kind of charm.

Where Rick was quiet and private, Tom was loud and full of life. The two of them couldn't have been more different, with the former preferring to spend his evenings at home, watching documentaries, and the latter spending his nights at poetry slams, strumming his guitar and writing in his notebook.

Since I hadn't been able to decide, I'd invited both of them to convince them of my plan. Given the amount of chemistry I had with the two of them, the only way to reach a satisfying conclusion was to sleep with the two of them.

At the same time.

Tom had brightened at the idea while Ricky slouched, some of the color draining from his face. Eventually, when I'd finally taken a seat, pulling a chair up with a screech and setting it at the head of the table, the two of them were sizing each other up.

"I think we should go back to my apartment and sort this out."

In silence, we'd made our way outside and into

the brusque evening air. Tom had taken my left side, a hint of spices and oranges clinging to his skin. Ricky, on the other hand, had smelled like sandalwood and sage, and he'd flanked my right side, brushing his hand against mine every so often.

A few blocks away, I'd led them up the stairs and stopped in front of the door.

I'd been so nervous, diary, I was sure I'd throw up then and there.

Instead, I took them inside and flicked the switch on and kicked off my shoes. By the time they'd settled on opposite sides of the couch, I'd peeled off my clothes and tossed them into a heap on the floor, leaving me in my red lace bra and underwear.

Ricky's mouth had fallen open.

Tom had leaned back against the couch, draping his arm over the back. "You look so sexy."

"Sexy enough for you to agree?" I'd sauntered over, stopping a few feet away. Then I'd given my hips a little extra sway before unhooking my bra. "I can't choose between the two of you, and this is the only way I know how."

Tom had shrugged and risen to his feet. "I'm down if you are."

With that, he'd pulled off his clothes, leaving him in his boxers. Moments later, he wandered over to me and tilted my head back. As soon as he kissed me, I'd thrown my head back, the knots in the center of my stomach unfurling. Tom had deepened the kiss, and my fingers linked over his head.

He sure did know how to take my breath away.

Warmth had pooled in the center of my stomach. Slowly, he'd leaned back to press hot, open-mouthed kisses along the side of my neck. His fingers had dug into my sides and pulled me against him. The length of him had brushed against me, and my knees had turned weak.

Until he'd lowered himself onto the floor and hooked a thumb underneath the waistband of my panties. His blue eyes had been bright and full of hunger as he slid them down over my legs and tossed them over my shoulders. Tom had pried my legs open and settled in between them, his mouth facing my center.

His tongue had darted in between my wet folds, sending me over the edge.

I'd wound my fingers through his hair and thrown my head back.

Tom had begun to make low, growling noises in the back of his neck when my eyes flew open. Out of the corner of my eye, I'd spotted Ricky getting up and taking off his shoes. His expression had turned relax, as if he was considering the whole thing more seriously. So I threw my head back and moaned. Tom's tongue continued to flick back and forth, stroking the bundle of nerves until I was shaking and panting his name.

As soon as I caught my breath, he'd stood up and kissed me soundly.

And so thoroughly I'd tasted myself on him.

Abruptly, he'd turned me around so I was facing Ricky. My eyes widened when he positioned himself behind me, and his arms came up on either side. He rubbed his hands up and down my arms while Ricky watched, his expression giving nothing away. Without warning, Ricky rose to his feet and peeled away his clothes. Once he was done, Tom entered me in one quick stroke.

I'd cried out his name so loudly I was sure the neighbors heard.

Over and over, we rocked back and forth against each other until my pulse quickened and a thin sheen of sweat broke out across my forehead. I threw my head back and wound my fingers through his hair. Tom sunk his teeth into my shoulders and made a low noise in the back of his throat that had shivers racing up and down my spine. When the force of my orgasm ripped through me, Tom had placed both hands around my stomach and squeezed.

He stayed inside of me until Ricky cleared his throat.

"Mind if I cut in?"

Tom had pressed a kiss to the back of my neck before easing out of me. With one last kiss, he strode over to the couch and lowered himself onto it. He spread his legs out on either side of him and stroked himself. Meanwhile, Ricky walked over to me and kissed me hard enough to make my toes curl. I'd swayed a little on my feet, the taste of soda and mint swirling around in my mouth.

When he drew back, he had the most intense look on his face.

With a wicked smile, I got down on my knees and kissed the tip of his member. Ricky made a low strangled noise, and his hands moved to the back of my head. He wound his fingers through my hair, drawing me closer to him.

I took him into my mouth and began to suck.

Ricky pumped in and out of my mouth, his face glistening with sweat. He dug his nails into my scalp and threw his head back. Moments later, I stopped and sat back on my legs. Then I stood up and cast a glance in Tom's direction. When I flipped my hair over my shoulders, I saw the two of them follow me.

It made me feel more powerful than I'd ever felt before, diary.

Like the two of them were going to fall to their knees and worship me.

With my heart hammering against my chest, I led them into my bedroom. Then I swallowed past the dryness in my throat, switched on the night lamp, and twisted to face them. I beckoned Ricky first and pushed him onto the mattress. I placed a leg on either side of him and cocked a finger in Tom's direction.

The bed dipped and creaked underneath him.

Tom placed his legs on either side of Ricky and glanced over my shoulders at him. A quick look passed between them before Ricky thrust upward. Moments later, when I was still adjusting on top of him, Tom thrust into me from the back.

Ricky's legs dangled over the edge of the bed.

As one, the two of them moved back and forth, easing out of me at an even, sensual pace. I threw my head back and squeezed my eyes, relishing every sensation that ricocheted through me. When Tom's hand came up around my breast, flicking the nipple, my hips bucked.

Then Ricky's hand went to the other breast, doing the same.

It wasn't long before my nipples were as hard as pebbles, and I began to bounce a little. Having both of them inside me at the same time was better than anything I could've imagined. Wave after wave of pleasure built up within me while I listened to the sound of their heavy breathing.

I don't think I've ever heard anything like that.

Once the smell of sweat and soap filled the room, my pulse quickened. I tried to keep my eyes open, to look at Ricky's handsome face, but I couldn't. Now and again, when I forced one eye open and saw the wild abandon on his face, I nearly collapsed on top of him. So I twisted my head to the side and stared at Tom, who gave me a heated look that had molten blood rushing through my veins.

I'd been expecting one of them to choke, or at the very least underperform under pressure. Unfortunately, not only were the two of them pounding into me like there was no tomorrow, but I was on the brink of another orgasm and still no closer to figuring out who was a better fit. Choosing based on who was better in the bedroom had seemed like a good idea at the time.

But all I'd been able to think about was how right

they both felt and how I wanted to stay like that until the world ended and our bones turned to dust. With wild and reckless abandon, the three of us moved together, moving closer and closer to an explosive climax.

Ricky tilted his head up and pressed his lips to mine.

I bit down on his bottom lip, and he growled.

Tom pressed both of my breasts together and sank his teeth into my neck. Dual waves of pain and pleasure rose within me, making my chest tighten. I curled my hands into fists on either side of the bed and blew out a deep, shaky breath.

The force of my third orgasm ripped through me, leaving me shaking violently. I writhed and spasmed, my lungs burning with effort. Tom gave a few more quick thrusts before pulling out and emptying himself onto the bed. Underneath, Ricky continued to thrust upwards, his thrusts growing harder and more frantic.

When he came, he jerked against me and went completely still.

Warmth pooled between my legs.

I rolled off of him and stared up at the ceiling.

Now, the two of them are sprawled on either side of the bed, with only a sheet to cover them. I'm hiding in the bathroom because I had to talk to someone, and I don't know who else to go to.

Last night didn't make anything clearer.

Instead, I'd discovered that they were both able to fuck me senseless.

So, diary, I think we're going to have to do it again a few times.

Just to be sure, you know.

Watermelon
Chrissy Lowell

"Are you sure about this?"

Kim sat up straighter and swung her gaze back to Kyle, who had a thin sheen of sweat on his forehead. He used the back of his hand to wipe his brow and blew out a breath. Then he stood up and after a few seconds of fanning himself, stripped off his shirt.

Revealing tanned and smooth muscles beneath.

Kim's mouth went dry. "Yeah, I'm sure. Why wouldn't I be?"

"Because it's a pretty big deal," Kyle replied with a slight shake of his head. "It's a pretty intimate thing."

Kim raised an eyebrow. "We've been together for two years, babe."

And she was more than ready to kick things up a notch.

As much as she loved Kyle, and the way he made her feel, she knew that they needed to try something different. While the sex between them still excited her and made her blood turn molten, they had been in a rut for a few months. Now and again, she found her mind wandering while he was on top of her, and she knew that something had to be done.

Which was why she had gone to Mary for help.

Usually, Mary was the one to talk her into doing crazy things, and over the years, Kim had learned to tune her out. Unfortunately, given the delicate nature of her situation, Kim knew she couldn't trust anyone else with this. Not when she had one shot to convince her sweet and nerdy boyfriend.

Kyle was eager to please her, and she took that as a good sign.

Slowly, she rose to her feet and dimmed the lights, casting the living room in a faint and eerie glow. Then she picked up her phone and issued a command, causing soft and sexy music to waft through the speakers overhead. In the distance, she heard the sound of tires screeching against asphalt and the howl of dogs, but she pushed it all away.

All she wanted was to focus on the man in front of her.

He was sitting with his hands folded in his lap, barefoot on the carpet, and with his jeans hanging low on his hips. His dark, unruly hair was tossed to the side, giving him a vulnerable and more boyish look. Wordlessly, Kim stripped down to her underwear and bra. Kyle's eyes widened in surprise.

"Shouldn't we talk about this some more?"

Kim shrugged and kicked her clothes away. "We can, but there's no reason we can't be comfortable. Why don't you take off your jeans?"

Kyle chuckled. "I know what you're trying to do."

Kim's hips swayed as she wandered over to him. She sat down on the couch and swung around to face them. Her eyes never left his face as she stretched her legs out in front of her and lifted her arms up over her head.

Kyle couldn't look away from her.

"I'm not trying to do anything. I'm succeeding," Kim teased in a low and husky voice. "You're over-thinking this. I'm trying to show you that you don't have to."

Kyle made a low noise in the back of his throat. "I don't want to hurt you."

Kim lowered her head and stared at him through lowered lashes. "I want you to hurt me. There's a difference."

Kyle swallowed heavily. "What if you don't like it?"

"What if I do?" Kim sat up and crawled toward him, aware of his heated gaze making her skin crawl with anticipation. She stopped a few feet away and reached for his glasses. Carefully, she set them down on the table behind him, brushing herself against him as she did. Kyle stopped breathing and went still.

When she sat back down, he took several deep breaths. "What if I don't like it?"

"We'll stop then," Kim suggested, her tongue darting out to lick her lips. "But we won't know until we try."

Abruptly, Kyle stood up and unbuttoned his jeans. He pushed them down his ankles before kicking them off. As soon as he sat back down, her eyes fell to the bulge in his pants, straining against the fabric of his boxers. Her heart began to hammer inside of her chest, and a shiver of anticipation raced through her.

Was this it?

She pressed her back against the couch and

brushed her hair out of her eyes. "Would it make you feel better if we had a safe word?"

Kyle paused and nodded slowly. "Yes."

"How about watermelon?"

Kyle threw his head back and laughed. "No offense, but it's a terrible safe word. Shouldn't you pick something else? Maybe something sexier."

Kim shrugged. "Why would I? This got your attention, didn't it? Besides, I like watermelons."

Although she doubted she was going to look at them the same after today.

Not that she minded.

Kyle stared at her for a few seconds before he covered the distance between them and kissed her. She sighed and linked her fingers over his neck. Before she could deepen the kiss, he drew back and ran a hand over his face.

"I want to tie you up," Kyle blurted out, his face turning a bright red. "I learned how to make knots when I was in the boy scouts...."

"I know."

"I'll make sure it's not too tight," Kyle added, his green eyes moving over her slowly, sensually. "I promise."

Kim nodded. "Okay."

Kyle searched her face. "There's still time to back out if you want to."

Kim stretched her entire body out on the coach and smiled. "Not a chance. How do you want me?"

Kyle swallowed and stood up. "Just like that. Hold on. I'll be right back."

With that, he bolted to his feet and disappeared down the hallway. Kim could hear her heart pounding against her ears. She sat up, reached for her half-full glass of water, and gulped it down. Then she flipped onto her side and placed a hand on her hips, striking a suggestive pose.

Kyle wouldn't know what hit him.

As soon as he returned, the butterflies in her stomach erupted, and she resisted the urge to move. He knelt down in front of her and touched his mouth to hers. Kyle tasted like mint toothpaste. She made a low, whimpering noise in the back of her throat and pushed herself closer. Suddenly, her hand darted between them, and she gripped him over the fabric of his boxers.

He made a low, strangled noise and wrenched his lips away. "I want to fuck you for a while."

Kim's eyes widened. "Okay."

"If things are going too far..."

Kim shook her head. "They aren't."

Flipping the tables on her and taking charge was sexy.

The last thing she'd expected was for Kyle to offer to tie her up. She had imagined him bending her over the couch and taking her then and there, without warning. By introducing rope into the mix, Kyle was heating things up, and it stoked something within her.

She had no idea he could be so domineering.

"Good." He motioned for her to sit up, and she did. The top of his head glistened underneath florescent lighting as he unwound his rope. His fingers moved quickly, deftly, like he had been doing this for a while. Before she knew what was happening, she found her feet firmly bound together. Then he took both of her hands in his and brought them up to his lips. Kyle took his time kissing each individual knuckle, letting his hot breath dance along the inside of her wrist before he sat back. With a wicked smile, he tied her hands together.

Kim tugged on the rope, and the low thrum in the center of her stomach turned molten. "I had no idea you were going to be this good."

"I had no idea you were going to look this sexy,"

Kyle replied in a husky voice. He knelt between them and nipped on her lower lip. She melted against him, fire rising up within her. When she parted her mouth to allow him access, Kyle's tongue slid in and began a sensual battle for dominance.

Every inch of her came alive.

She shifted, trying to pull him closer and pulled against her restraints. "Don't you want to come closer?"

Kyle's mouth moved down, pressing hot, open-mouthed kisses along the side of her neck. He stopped at her breasts and took one nipple between his teeth. Her pulse jumped when he licked and sucked until her hips bucked. Then he switched his attention to the other one, lavishing it with the same amount of attention so they were both as hard as pebbles.

Once he pulled back, Kim made a low, whimpering noise.

She burned for him.

His gaze was searing when he moved back to look at her. "Should I stop?"

Kim shook her head. "Never."

Abruptly, Kyle reached for her bound legs and threw them over his shoulders, so his mouth was at her center. He blew, his hot breath doing strange things to her insides. When his tongue darted out, in between her wet folds, Kim cried out. She threw her head back and cried out his name.

"I'm just getting started," Kyle promised in between licks. He pressed his hands on either side of her and growled. "You taste amazing, Kim."

Kim gasped when his tongue began to swipe back and forth. "Oh, Kyle. Oh, yes."

"Yes what?"

"Yes, just like that."

"Like this?" Kyle gripped the edges of her feet and made a low noise in the back of his throat. He began to alternate between sucking her and licking back and forth, leaving her writhing and panting beneath him. She squeezed her eyes and ground against him, relishing every wave of pleasure that built up within her. Her eyes squeezed shut, and she dug her nails into the inside of her palms.

Wave after wave of pleasure rose up within her.

Sweat formed on the back of her neck and slid down the length of her back. Kyle's hands shifted, and he pressed her breasts together, sending another jolt through her. She made a low humming noise.

All at once, she was falling, the force of her pleasure ripping through her. Her eyes flew open, and spots danced in her field of vision. Kim's body writhed and spasmed while she gasped, her chest tightening with emotion. As soon as she could breathe again, her vision cleared, and Kyle lowered her legs. He knelt forward and kissed her, the taste of her juices strong on his lips. She sighed, and one arm traveled to the back of her neck, massaging the skin there. He framed her face in his hands, and his kiss turned gentle.

"Keep going," Kim pleaded breathlessly. "I don't want you to stop."

Kyle gave her another kiss before leaning back. He stood up and helped her to her feet. Then he swept her into his arms and took her into the kitchen. Slowly, he set her down on her feet and pulled out a chair with a screech. His heavy breathing reverberated inside of her head. With a smile, he brought the chair to a rest against the counter. Gently, he spun her around so her back was facing him. Her chest came to a rest against the front of the chair, her butt dangling off the edge of the seat.

He lowered himself onto the floor and untied her feet.

Without wasting any time, he tied her ankles to the feet of the chair. His breath was hot in her ear as he untied her hands and pulled them behind her back. In a few quick and nimble movements, he tied her wrists together and pressed a kiss between her shoulder blades.

Goosebumps broke out across her flesh.

She heard him suck a in harsh breath, and her breath hitched in her throat. He ran his fingers down the length of her back and stopped at her behind. Then he used one hand to stroke the smooth skin there while the other messaged her scalp. Little pinpricks of desire burst through her, making her chest tighten.

"You have no idea how hot you are right now." Kyle's mouth moved over her flushed skin, leaving a trail of heat in his wake. He stopped when he reached the dip of her back and sat down. Moments later, she felt him brush himself against her, and her knees turned weak.

In one quick thrust, he was inside of her.

Kyle went absolutely still as her muscles contracted and expanded, taking in every inch of him. When she released a deep sigh, he began to move inside of her, his grunts and groans like music to her ears. The chair creaked and groaned underneath her. Through the thin walls of their apartment, she heard a TV, and the volume went up. Her lips lifted into a half smile as she shifted, trying to buck against him.

"Fuck, you feel so good, Kim." Kyle leaned forward and spoke directly into her ear, causing shivers to raise up and down her spine. "You're so tight and wet."

"I love being dominated by you," Kim said in a strangled voice. "Oh, Kyle. Oh, God."

He growled into her ear. "You like it when I'm dirty, don't you?"

"Yes," Kim ground out in between pants. "Oh, yes."

"Yeah, baby. You like it rough," Kyle continued in a voice that made the butterflies in her stomach erupt. "I like it when you beg for me."

"Oh, please."

Kyle eased out and slammed back into her. "Please what?"

"Please, Kyle." Kim squeezed her eyes shut, rivulets of sweat sliding down her back and the sides of her face. "Please don't stop."

Kyle made a guttural sound in the back of his throat. "I'm not going to stop. I could do this all night, baby."

"Yes," Kim breathed. "We should."

Kyle eased in and out of her in long, practiced strokes. First, he circled his hips, then he began to push upwards, hitting her sweet spot over and over. By the time another wave washed over her, Kim couldn't stop chanting his name. Her entire body shook and spasmed. He brought his head to a rest against her back and grew still. Then he untied her ankles and her arms.

She touched her wrists and spun around to kiss him, pouring every ounce of emotion she had into it. He responded by hoisting her up and carrying her into the bedroom. There, he set her down on the bed, his eyes staying on her face. Then he spun her around so her back was facing his and began to rub his hands up and down her arms. Then he tied her wrists together, giving the rope a firm tug before he moved down to her feet.

Without warning, he tied the left ankle to the right thigh and tied the left thigh to the left upper arm bicep. She twisted her head, and his lips found hers, soft and gentle. He moved his mouth against hers and shifted. When he turned her head to the front, she was facing the blue colored wall on the other side of the room.

Kyle eased into her from the back.

She blew out a breath. "This feels amazing."

Kyle kissed the back of her neck. "You're completely at my mercy."

"I am."

Kyle dug his fingers into her hips and circled. "Do you want me to go slow?"

Kim threw her head back and moaned. "Yes."

Abruptly, he slid out of her and slid back in again. "Are you sure about that?"

"I don't care. As long as you fuck me."

Kyle pressed a kiss between her shoulder blades, making the hairs on the back of her neck rise. "I love it when you talk dirty to me."

With a deep exhale, he buried his face in the crook of her neck and moved inside of her. She rocked back and forth against him, angling her body so he hit all the right spots. When his hands came up from behind and pushed her breasts together, she thought she was going to explode. Every part of her came alive and felt like it was on fire for him.

He flicked one nipple then the other.

Kim continued to stare at the spot on the wall and moan.

The bed creaked and groaned underneath him, the sound echoing in the stillness of the room. Kyle drew out of her and brought his hand to a rest against her hips. He slapped one butt cheek and the other before thrusting back in. Dual waves of pain and pleasure ricocheted through her. Her breathing turned into sharp little puffs as she struggled against her bindings.

"Don't cum yet," Kyle said directly into her. "I want you to hold it, Kim. Do you understand?"

She nodded. "I do."

He dug his nails into either side of her hips and pulled her against him. The smell of sweat and soap filled the room. He drew his mouth back, his hot breath dancing across her skin. When he sank his teeth into her shoulders, Kim jerked back and cried out. Kyle held her still against him and continued to pump into her, pushing her closer and closer to the edge.

Kim came undone with a violent spasm.

As soon as she regained her breath, Kyle gave a few quick thrusts, and warmth pooled between her legs. He went still against her, his breathing even. Slowly, his fingers moved over the rope, releasing her arms and legs. Once he did, she flipped onto her side and curled against him. With a smile, Kyle threw an arm over her shoulders and tucked her into his side.

"Where did you learn how to do that? The boy scouts definitely didn't teach you that."

Kyle chuckled and pressed a kiss to the top of her

head. "Research. You've been dropping hints all week."

Kim looked up at him and smiled. "Want to show me more of that research?"

Kyle tilted her head back and kissed her. "We've got all night, baby."

Wild Ella
By Clifford Brannum

"You really went all-out tonight," Ella giggled, heat rushing up her cheeks. She peeled off her coat and draped it over her hand, her eyes darting around the candlelit room expectantly. "Are you sure your parents aren't going to come back?"

Caleb pulled her toward him. "They're out of town for the night. We have the house all to ourselves."

Ella tilted her head back, her blue eyes bright and mischievous. "Good."

Caleb claimed her mouth with his.

He'd been waiting a long time for this night.

She shuddered and melted against him, tasting like strawberry lip gloss and mint mouthwash. When she tilted her head to the side, he nipped on her lower lip, and her mouth parted.

His pulse quickened when her arms came up around his shoulders and squeezed.

All the blood rushed to his cock.

Slowly, Ella drew away from him and pushed her hair out of her face. "Why don't we get more comfortable?"

Caleb's heart hammered against his chest. "Sure."

With that, he led her toward the couch, barefoot over the wooden floorboards. He came to a stand in front of the couch and motioned for her to sit. Then he wandered over to the fireplace, bent down, and stoked the flames. They jumped and crackled, casting long, orange red shadows across the wall. Outside, the cold wind whistled and howled. Through the curtain, Caleb saw the crescent-shaped moon and smiled.

He was going to rock Ella's world, and she had no idea.

Not only were his parents gone for two whole days, but with the whole house to themselves and an excuse for Ella in place, the two of them were finally free to be together. He'd been dreaming about this night for months. Given that they'd been dating for an entire year, Caleb had done a good job of being patient, but he was about ready to explode.

And he wanted to lose himself in Ella.

She came up behind him, knelt down in front of the fire, and held up her hands. "I love this."

"I know how much you love fireplaces," Caleb murmured before pressing a kiss to her cheeks. "I also got us some wine."

Ella smiled and pressed her lips to his. "You really did think of everything."

Caleb stood up and pulled her to his feet. He wrapped his arms around her waist, and she tilted her head back to look up at him. "I want tonight to be special."

Ella blushed. "Me too."

As soon as he claimed his mouth with hers, she made a low whimpering noise and threaded her fingers through his hair. He couldn't believe how much he wanted her, needed to be inside of her. One hand stayed on her waist, and the other traveled up, stopping at the back of her neck. He kneaded the muscles there, and she shivered.

Holy shit.

He couldn't wait to feel every inch of her skin pressed against his.

Impatiently, he maneuvered them backwards

until they reached the couch. Ella lowered herself onto it with a low, whimpering sound. Reluctantly, he wrenched his lips away and pulled his shirt up over his head. With a smile, he tossed it over his shoulder and waited till it fell with a flutter. Ella fumbled with the zipper on the front of her hoodie.

Caleb sat down and helped her, letting the tight fabric fall behind her.

In the soft light, her skin glistened, and she had a warm glow around her. Caleb's heartbeat quickened as he reached for her and framed his face in her hands. She kissed him back slowly, gently, as if they had all the time in the world. One hand stayed on the back of her neck, and the other moved up and down her arms, leaving a trail of heat in its wake.

Ella drew him closer.

Once she fell backwards against the couch, Caleb draped himself over her, her bra the only barrier between them. He ran his fingers along her tan, smooth skin and stopped at the hook. Her mouth parted when he fumbled with it, managing to get it undone after some grunting. Abruptly, she sat up, pressed her arms together, and pulled it off.

His eyes moved over her face before sliding down to her breasts.

Round, perky, and full.

Just like they always were.

Caleb's mouth watered as Ella lowered herself back onto the couch and pushed her dark hair out of her eyes. Her lips spread into a slow, sultry smile, and all of his blood rushed south. In the back of his throat, he made a guttural sound before lowering his head. He took one nipple between his teeth and tugged.

She tasted like butter and vanilla.

His eyes rolled to the back of his head as she moaned, linking her fingers behind his neck. She wrapped her legs around his waist as he moved to the other breast and pinned her arms over her head. Ella's gasp of surprise made his cock twitch. He rubbed himself against her, and she bucked, a thin sheen of sweat breaking out across her forehead.

"Shit. You have no idea how badly I want to fuck you right now," Caleb breathed, pausing to blow out a breath. "I can't wait to be balls deep inside of you."

Ella's eyes flew open, and she stared at him through lowered lashes. "I want you too, Caleb."

His fingers moved to the zipper of her jeans. "Let me get these damn clothes off."

Ella took her hand in his and sat up. "Not like this."

Caleb glanced up at her. "What do you mean?"

"I want to wait till I'm married, remember?"

"You're joking, right?"

"No, I've been telling you for months. I wasn't trying to be sexy or playing hard to get. I want to be a virgin when I get married."

Caleb frowned. "So what are we going to do?"

"We can still have fun, Caleb," Ella replied with a smile. "Okay?"

"Okay."

Ella palmed him over the thin fabric of his jeans and squeezed. "You don't sound convinced."

Caleb rubbed himself against her. "I just want you so badly."

Ella covered the distance between them and kissed him hard. "You can still have me."

Caleb growled into her mouth, "I want to fuck you, Ella. And I know you want to fuck me too."

Ella made a low choking noise and pressed herself against him. Caleb moved his hands up and down her bare arms, leaving goosebumps in his wake. He dug his nails into her waist, and she murmured his name. Suddenly, Ella drew back and stood up. Her eyes never left his face as she unbuttoned her jeans and slid them down her legs. Once they pooled at her ankles, she stepped out of them, revealing lacy black underwear underneath. Caleb's mouth fell open when she spun around, bent over, and pulled her underwear down over her tight, toned ass.

She wheeled back around to face him. Caleb had dug his palms into the couch, his erection straining painfully against his boxers. Wordlessly, Ella came to stand in front of him, completely naked, placed one leg on either side of him, and settled on his lap, the smell of her sweet juices wafting up his nostrils. Caleb placed a hand on her waist, and the other brushed her hair out of her face.

"Tell me what you want, baby," Caleb whispered into her skin.

Ella ground against him. "I want to feel you."

Caleb lifted his hips up off the couch and rubbed himself against her. "How's this?"

Ella threw her head back and moaned, the sound echoing in his ears. "Fuck, that feels so good."

Caleb placed his other hand on her waist and squeezed. "How about now?"

Ella blew out a breath. "You feel so good."

Caleb buried his face in her neck and breathed. "Fuck, Ella. I don't know how to control myself around you."

Ella lifted herself up and ground against him, harder this time.

His cock pulsed and twitched.

Ella linked her fingers through his hair and drew his head back. She pressed him against her chest and bounced up and down. He squeezed his eyes shut and took a nipple between his teeth. Caleb's mouth darted between the two until they were both as hard as pebbles. As soon as they were, his hand darted between them and slipped in between her slick, wet folds.

Her juices immediately coated his hand.

She cried out and bucked against him.

He pushed another finger in and wasted no time finding her sweet spot. Ella dug her fingers into his shoulders and rocked against him. The couch creaked and dipped underneath them. Ella came a short while later, writhing and spasming against him. Her muscles expanded and contracted while his fingers continued to move. Once she caught her breath, he removed his fingers and looked at her.

As soon as her eyes cleared, he placed both fingers in his mouth and sucked. "You taste good."

Ella leaned between them and pressed her lips to his. "So do you."

Caleb swallowed. "What now?"

On shaky legs, Ella stood up and gathered her hair up off the nape of her neck. "You can get rid of those clothes."

Caleb was on his feet in an instant and pulling at his jeans. They fell to the floor with a flutter, joining the pile of clothes there. His hands were clumsy and sweaty as he pulled his boxers down and stood up to face her. Ella's eyes traveled over him, starting at the top of his head and stopping at his enlarged manhood. She paused, and her eyes widened slightly. When her tongue darted out to lick her lips, Caleb balled his hands into fists at his sides.

Although the evening was not going how he'd hoped, Caleb knew he wouldn't want to be anywhere else. Especially when Ella approached him and knelt down on the carpeted floor. On her knees, she sat back on her legs and looked up at him. Slowly, she leaned forward so her mouth was inches away from his member.

Ella began to lick him, and he growled, "Yes, baby. I love how your mouth feels on me."

She made a noise of agreement in the back of her throat and placed one hand on either side of his thighs. Quickly, she shifted so she took all of him. Her tongue moved quickly and deftly, bringing him closer and closer to the edge. He cupped the back of her neck and squeezed firmly. Ella glanced up at him and stopped. Suddenly, he pulled her to her knees, and she pressed herself against him.

"I want to be inside of you," Caleb told her, dark eyes moving intently over her face. "I know you want to be a virgin, and I respect that, but I need to be inside of you or I'm going to go crazy."

Ella nodded and kissed him.

Before he could deepen the kiss, Ella turned around and bent over so her ass was in the air. She looked over at him and gave him a wicked smile that made the blood on his veins pound. He stroked her back and licked his mouth.

"I want you to fuck me in the ass," Ella told him in a husky voice.

"What?"

Ella wriggled against him, her smile growing wider. "I know you've thought about it. Don't you want to have fun?"

Caleb cleared his throat. "Well, yeah, but isn't it kind of painful?"

Ella shook her head. "Not if you do it right."

Caleb positioned himself behind her and stopped. "Are you sure?"

"There's some water-based lubricant in my bag," Ella replied, swinging her gaze back to the front. "It'll help."

Caleb took a few steps back and fumbled in the semi-darkness until his hand closed around her backpack. In the front pocket, he found the tube and held it up to the flickering light. He squeezed a generous amount onto his finger and went to stand behind Ella. Using two fingers, he rubbed the lube all over himself, his fingers slick and clumsy. Ella was already touching herself and moaning.

Uncertainly, he came to stand behind her and thrust forward. "I don't think it's working."

Ella twisted her arms behind her back, stopping a few inches away from his member. "Can you see it?"

Caleb peered at her behind. "Yes."

"You have to aim for it," Ella murmured in a hoarse voice. "Can you do that?"

Caleb cleared his throat and tried again, but he kept missing. He made a low, frustrated noise and stepped back. "I don't think I can do this."

Ella craned her neck over her shoulders and smiled at him. "Yes, you can. I'll help you."

Caleb smirked. "I wasn't aware you were such an expert."

Ella chuckled. "I'm not, but I know my way around. Okay, can you see me properly?"

"Yes."

"Position yourself behind me and ease in," Ella

instructed, her voice rising toward the end. "Don't go in all at once."

Caleb blew out a breath, took a few steps forward, and did as he was told. When the tip went in, he went still and cursed. "Fuck, that feels so good."

"We're just getting started," Ella promised in a throaty voice. "Now ease out of me and slam back in."

Caleb gripped her hips, eased out, and thrust back in. "Like this?"

Ella bucked against him, and her head twisted to the front. "Exactly."

With a grunt, Caleb dug his nails into her waist and rocked back and forth against her. She bucked against him, mumbling incoherently into the darkness. Suddenly, she twisted to face him, and the look on her face nearly had him exploding. Ella licked her lips and cleared her throat.

"I want you to go in deeper," Ella whispered. "Keep thrusting in and out of me, but each time, go deeper."

Caleb grunted in agreement and sucked in a deep breath. Over and over, he thrust in and out of her, pushing himself farther in each time. As soon as he was all the way in, Ella went completely still and let out a deep, shaky breath. Suddenly, she began to grind against him with wild and reckless abandon.

He brought his head to a rest against her glistening, flushed back. "You're so tight, Ella. Fuck."

"Oh, Caleb. You're so big." Ella threw her head back and moaned. Out of the corner of his eye, he saw her hand move and dart in between her wet folds. His blood began to roar in his ears when he heard the familiar sounds of her pleasure reverberating inside of his head. Abruptly, Ella's hand darted out, and she placed one hand on either side of her thighs.

Caleb stood up straighter and circled his hips. "Is this how you want to be fucked?"

Ella let out a deep, throaty moan. "Oh, yes."

Caleb's nails dug into her waist, keeping her in place. "Good because I want to keep fucking you, Ella. I hope you're ready because we're going to be up all night."

"Oh, Caleb."

"That's it," he coaxed roughly. "That's a good girl."

"Harder," Ella pleaded in a strangled voice. "Please."

Caleb brought his head to a rest against the small

of her back and blew out a breath. "You're not so innocent, are you? You like it dirty, don't you, Ella?"

Ella cried out his name. "I like you fucking me."

Caleb growled into her back, "Good because I plan on doing this all the time."

Ella bit back her whimper.

"Don't hold back," Caleb said, drawing back. His hands moved forward, and he played with her nipples. "I want to hear you. I want to hear you while I'm fucking you, Ella."

"The neighbors," Ella gasped when his hand came up over her center and squeezed. She bucked against him and began to chant his name. He pushed one finger then another and thrust into her. Ella rocked back and forth against him, her movements wild and reckless. Together, the two of them moved, inching closer and closer to the edge.

Caleb squeezed his eyes shut and enjoyed the feel of her, pulsing and writhing around him. She was tight and wet and much better than anything he'd imagined. He soon found her sweet spot, and he stroked. When she began to moan, he pressed his face against her back and grunted.

She came undone with a violent shudder, rocking and spasming against him. He held her still while she rode out her high, his rhythm turning slow and pronounced. Ella caught her breath as he held her up by her ass and thrust deeply inside of her. She gasped and held still.

He eased in and out of her in long, practiced strokes.

Ella ground against him, the sound of her whimpers like music to his ears. Eventually, she twisted her arms over her back and reached for him. He leaned into it and pressed his lips together. She wound her fingers through his hair and tugged, sending dual waves of pain and pleasure in quick succession.

Her cries echoed off the walls, making the blood in his veins boil.

Suddenly, his entire body seized and jerked. He groaned, pouring himself into her while she stroked his hair. Ella was panting and still as he rode out his high. Once his breath returned to normal, she shifted, and he eased out of her. She drew him into her arms and held him to her as they both shuddered.

Slowly, she leaned back to looked up at him. "How was it?"

Caleb gave her a weak smile and kissed her forehead. "You have to teach me more."

Ella chuckled. "You got it."

Christine's First Gangbang
By Richard Kinney

"I can't believe this is actually happening!" Christine squealed, bouncing up and down as she clapped her hands together. "Thank you so much, Matt, really! You're the best!"

"I am," Matt agreed easily, smirking as he wrapped an arm around her waist and pulled her close to prevent her from running inside just yet. "Now promise me that you'll remember my one and only rule for the night."

"Of course, I promise." Christine nodded quickly. "The last man who gets to cum inside me tonight... will be you."

"Good girl." Matt leaned down to plant a kiss on her lips, patting her behind a few times before opening the door for her. "Let's go."

Christine giggled, smiling so widely that her cheeks were beginning to get sore as the two of them walked inside.

Matt had finally agreed to bring her to the sex club that they'd been hearing rave reviews about for the longest time, and Christine was already over the moon with happiness! She'd always wanted to pay a visit to a sex club, but before she'd started dating Matt, she'd never had anyone that she felt safe enough with.

Thankfully, she and Matt had managed to build a relationship filled with trust and mutual respect, so she was completely comfortable being here with him tonight, and he was fully comfortable with helping her finally fulfill her long-time dream of getting gangbanged.

It had been one of Christine's biggest fantasies for as long as she could remember—being surrounded by cocks, manhandled, used like nothing more than a fuck toy by men that she didn't even know—but she hadn't been able to make it happen until now, and it was all thanks to Matt.

He'd been a little iffy about it when she'd first told him that it was something that she wanted to try, but the more he thought about it, the more he liked the idea of watching his girlfriend being used by men that he got to handpick himself. He was a bit of a sadist, not to mention a voyeur, so this was right up his alley.

Besides, Christine had an insatiable hunger for sex, and as much as he hated to admit it, sometimes Matt found himself struggling to keep up. But if all went well tonight, the two of them would be making frequent trips back to the sex club, and Christine would be able to wear herself out with a whole flock of cocks as often as she pleased. This was a win for them both.

The inside of the club was lively and somewhat intimidating to newcomers like themselves. The first thing they saw upon walking in was several women in cages around the room, some of them masturbating, some of them pole-dancing, all of them naked. There were velvet couches all around. Some people sat watching the women perform, others seemed to be participating in one giant orgy.

Matt's cock twitched as his eyes trailed the large room for a few seconds before he forced himself to look away in order to locate the hallway that led to the more private rooms.

There were still plenty of people inside, they noticed once they walked inside of one, but there were significantly fewer people than there were in the main area.

Matt wore a proud smile as heads turned and eyes caught on the beautiful woman that was standing next to him. Christine was drop-dead gorgeous, if you asked him. Her long, wavy blond hair, green eyes, and petite yet curvy body always seemed to draw attention wherever they went, and tonight, she was only wearing an all-black lingerie set, having decided to forgo picking out an outfit when she knew it'd only be ripped off her anyway.

She looked like a model, and Matt could tell by the way some of the men perked up and eyed her curiously that they were interested in getting a piece of her.

Perfect.

Matt took his time scanning the room, trying to find just the right men for the job. When he caught sight of a group of five big, muscular men who all seemed to be eye-fucking Christine as they pointed and talked about her, he grabbed her hand and began dragging her over to them, wearing an easy smile as he approached them.

"Hey." He tried not to sound so awkward as he sent them a wave. "I'm Matt, and this is my girl-friend, Christine."

"Hey," one of them greeted, licking his lips as he eyed the suddenly shy-looking girl, who was trying her best to hide behind Matt's back, though he pulled her to stand in front of him once he noticed.

"Would any of you guys happen to be up for a gangbang tonight?" Matt decided to just cut straight to the chase. "Christine doesn't mind begging if you guys are into that, but if not, we can find some other guys–"

"No, no, no, we're definitely into it," one of them chuckled. "I think it's safe to say that we'd all be down for a gangbang. I'm Liam, by the way, and this is Dean, Nolan, Colton, and Dominic–not that it matters much, huh?" He smirked as he eyed Christine, his eyes catching on her small breasts for a moment before trailing back up to her face. "So Christine is a free-use slut and you're like her owner, right?"

Christine's cheeks turned bright red as she turned to look at Matt, who was no stranger to the obvious look of arousal swirling around in her eyes. He let out a fond chuckle, squeezing her hip with a bruising grip as he looked at the guys and nodded.

"Yeah, that sounds about right."

"Nice," Dean said, gesturing for them to follow him toward a nearby couch. "So anything we should know before we start? Any rules and boundaries to keep in mind?"

"There isn't much that she doesn't like." Matt shrugged his shoulders. "She likes it rough. Choking, slapping, hair-pulling, spitting, spanking, biting, scratching–the whole nine. Do whatever you want, but her safe word is 'Gymnastics,' and if she can't talk, she'll tap you six times if she wants you to stop. Oh–and try to keep all her holes filled at all times. She gets whiny when she's empty for more than a couple of seconds. Here–do you mind if I watch from the couch while you guys fuck her on the floor? It's where she belongs anyway."

"No problem," Nolan said, already tugging her panties off. The rest of them were already naked–another reason why Matt had decided to go up to them. They were all hung. "Is she already prepped and stretched?"

"Yep." Matt grinned. "She was so excited to come here today that she spent a couple of hours getting herself ready last night. She looked so cute begging for me to fist her."

"Fisting?" Liam raised his brows, eyeing the girl who was now being fondled by Colton and Dean. The two of them both had one of her breasts in hand, squeezing them as Nolan kicked her legs apart and pushed three fingers inside her cunt.

"She's sturdier than she looks," Matt stated simply, yanking down his sweats before taking a seat on the couch.

Christine's eyes fluttered shut as she listened to her boyfriend talking about her as if she wasn't even there. She was already dripping wet, which Nolan commented on with a quiet chuckle as he pulled his fingers out of her cunt and pushed them inside of her mouth. She opened her eyes again, staring at him as she sucked on his fingers eagerly, and the men surrounding her hooted and laughed as they repositioned her, putting her on her knees.

"I want her mouth first. She looks like she gives good blowjobs," Colton commented.

"How come you always get to have first dibs?" Dominic grumbled under his breath.

"Oh, yeah, I forgot to mention, don't hesitate to share one hole between two cocks," Matt chuckled. "She can handle it."

"Wow, we really lucked out tonight," Liam murmured as he pranced over to them, wordlessly sliding down to the ground and pushing Christine's knees apart. He lay down on his back, wrapping his arms around her thighs and pulling her down until she was sitting on his face, and she gasped as his tongue immediately began trailing between her folds.

Matt began stroking himself slowly as he watched Colton grab Christine's hair and pull her head forward. She dutifully opened her mouth, easily welcoming his large girth inside. He moved his hips slowly, pushing his cock all the way to the back of her throat before pulling out until only the tip of it was still inside her mouth. Dominic pushed the tip of his cock inside as well, clearly surprised by the fact that she was able to fit them both.

"Holy shit," Dean groaned as he tilted his head. "Look how pretty she looks with two cocks in her mouth...Where did you find a girlfriend like this?!"

"I guess I lucked out as well," Matt chuckled.

Christine moaned, grinding against Liam's face as she stared up at the two men with their cocks in her mouth. Her jaw was already starting to ache, and her lips burned from being stretched so wide, but she loved the feeling. She loved the way her drool leaked from her mouth and over her exposed breasts too. When the two of them both pulled out, she furrowed her brows in confusion until Dominic pushed his entire length back inside before pulling out and allowing Colton to do the same.

The two of them started up a steady rhythm, taking turns fucking her face as she held her mouth open and tried her best not to gag around their massive cocks. Meanwhile, Liam was still eating her out like a man that had been starved. Christine's eyes rolled back as he made her continue to slide back and forth over his face, tongue-fucking her quickly. She was already quivering as her first orgasm of the night rapidly approached.

She was always quick to cum, so Matt wasn't surprised to see her trembling through an orgasm just a couple of minutes later, the lower half of Liam's face soaked once he pulled himself off from under her with a pleased smile.

Just a few minutes after that, Colton and Dominic reached their peak too. Colton shoved his cock into her mouth one final time, ordering her not to swallow until they gave her permission as he came down her throat. Dominic managed to hold out until he was finished, but the moment Colton pulled out, Dominic began stroking himself quickly, groaning as he watched his seed land all over Christine's tongue.

"Shit," Nolan mumbled as he stared at her,

watching as some of the cum dripped off her tongue and onto the ground, but she still held her mouth open as she'd been told to. It wasn't until after both Colton and Dominic had spit inside her mouth that they gave her permission to swallow, which she did, happily. The sight drew a low groan out of Nolan, who immediately called next dibs on her mouth.

Liam grabbed Christine by her hair, forcing her to crawl behind him as he walked over to Dean. "Why don't the two of us share her ass and pussy while Nolan uses her mouth?"

"You know I'm not going to say no to that," Dean chuckled, pulling Christine up by the arm. "You get behind her, I'll get in front."

Liam nodded wordlessly, spinning the girl around until she was facing away from him and pressed against Dean. She gasped, letting out a startled squeak as he hiked one of her legs up until Dean rested the palm of his hand beneath her thigh to hold it up himself. Liam pushed down on her back, forcing her to arch it and lean closer to Dean while he pressed the head of his cock against her ass hole.

Christine bit her lip as he slid inside in one quick motion. She was hardly used to the feeling of his large cock stretching her ass when Dean slipped inside of her cunt, letting out a slew of curses as he felt her warm heat wrapped around his cock.

"Oh my God," she practically whispered as she clung to Dean, resting her forehead against his shoulder as the two of them began slowly thrusting in and out of her. She didn't get to rest there for long before her body was being twisted slightly and she was forced to bend forward until she was face to cock. Nolan tapped the tip of his cock against her lips until she opened her mouth and welcomed him inside.

The position was uncomfortable for Christine, whose muscles were already starting to sting and burn, but she didn't mind it if it meant getting to please three different cocks at once—four when Dominic came over to get a handjob after getting it up again.

Christine was overwhelmed as Dean and Liam took turns pounding into her quickly. Her ass was still sore from yesterday when Matt had fisted her, and her pussy was already sensitive from her first orgasm, so she was already feeling thoroughly used. On top of that, she was hyperaware of the fact that her own boyfriend was watching her as she was shared between the large men, and he wasn't the only one watching. She could feel the stares of the other people in the room burning into her skin as they all watched, getting themselves off while they did.

Matt was aware of it too. He couldn't wipe the smug expression off his face as he eyed the twenty or so other men in the room while they stared in awe at his girlfriend. It seemed to be an unspoken rule not to impose on a scene that you hadn't been asked to be a part of, so none of them approached her, which Matt was grateful for. But he could see how badly they wanted to join in on the fun, and he was already taking note of who he'd like to see fuck her next time.

Christine was preoccupied enough as it was for now, though, and Matt quickly turned his attention back to her when he heard her muffled moans becoming more frequent. Like clockwork, she came after just a couple of minutes, and the men continued fucking her afterward, even as she tried to squirm away from them. Nolan emptied his load inside her mouth a few minutes later, and she swallowed every drop of his cum just as eagerly as she'd swallowed Colton's and Dominic's earlier.

Dean was next to cum, pulling out of her cunt in order to paint her face with his seed instead, but when Liam came, he remained balls deep inside her ass, making sure that not a drop of it slid out until he pulled out of her and allowed her to collapse to the ground, free for someone else to use next.

Dominic and Colton both decided to share her cunt. Dominic was already close because of the handjob that she'd given him, but he'd been holding out just so he could have the chance to fuck her gaping cunt, and Colton wasn't about to miss out on the chance to double penetrate someone when he'd never had the opportunity to do so before, so he was quick to slide in alongside Dominic.

Christine cried out as her pussy was stretched while she slowly sank down on the two of their cocks. She barely had the strength to move by that point, and it was all she could do to hold herself up while the two of them pounded into her quickly. Colton grabbed her hand and forced her to rub her clit even as she cried and whined about being too sensitive to touch herself, chuckling as she sniffled and sobbed while slowly rubbing circles over the swollen nub.

Matt had stopped touching himself long ago, and now he was clutching the base of his cock tightly to keep himself from cumming untouched as he watched. He'd majorly underestimated just how hot getting to watch this would be. At this point, he couldn't believe that there had ever been a time when he'd been hesitant to agree to this, even if it was brief.

Christine ended up squirting twice before Colton and Dominic came, and by the time the two of them pulled out in order to cum all over her stomach, she could hardly find the strength to move, but she pulled herself to sit up with a look of determination on her face anyway. She had made a promise, after all.

Matt crooned at her, smiling as she gingerly crawled over to him and climbed into his lap with a quiet groan. "Your turn," she murmured, already burying her face in the crook of his neck sleepily.

Matt easily slid inside her loose cunt, letting out a sigh of relief as he finally got to be inside of his girlfriend for the first time tonight. "Such a good girl," he complimented, stroking her hair as he fucked into her with shallow thrusts. "You were a star tonight! You know you look gorgeous while you're pleasing a bunch of cocks, right?"

Christine grunted, and that was as much of a response as Matt was going to get. He chuckled as he squeezed her closer to him, hugging her as he continued fucking her sloppy cunt until he came.

He was smug as he spilled inside of her, satisfied by the longing looks on everyone else's faces. He was the only one who had the privilege of cumming inside of her pussy, and the only one who ever would. It was a reminder, for him and for her and for everybody else as well, that no matter how many other men she fucked, she would always truly belong to him and him only.

The Massage
By Marine Leland

"Fuck," Sherry practically mewled, her body melting into the mattress as her muscles finally relaxed for what felt like the first time in centuries. "Right there! Fuck, yes, that feels so good!" she moaned when Lucy's fingers began digging into the right side of her neck.

"Sherry," Lucy giggled as she tried to fight off the blush that was threatening to cover her cheeks. She was thankful that Sherry was lying face down, unable to see what a flustered mess she was becoming. "I've barely even touched you yet!"

"Yeah, but your fingers are literally magical!" Sherry fussed in between moans. "I've been here for like three minutes, and already my body feels like a cloud. I haven't felt this light since I was a ten-year-old without a worry in the world aside from how to convince my mom to buy me my fifth Barbie lunchbox of the school year. Why have you been keeping your hidden talent a secret from me, your supposed best friend?!"

"You're so dramatic." Lucy snorted. "And is a hidden talent really a hidden talent if it's not a secret? Telling people about it defeats the whole purpose. Besides, every time I mention that I'm good at giving massages, people start expecting them from me all the time. My biggest mistake in life is telling my sister's big, dumb boyfriend about the massage therapy classes I took a few years ago. Now I'm stuck working the kinks out of his hairy back every other weekend unless I want to hear my sister's guilt-tripping."

"No, I'd say your biggest mistake in life was telling me about the massage therapy classes." Sherry grinned after lifting her head and turning to look back at Lucy. "Now I'm gonna have to test your knowledge. Thoroughly. I'm thinking we'll have to schedule a couple of sessions per week. Three massages at the minimum!"

Lucy smirked and pushed Sherry's head back down without a word. She wasn't quite sure what to say to that. It wasn't as if she'd mind it if they really made that a thing anyway. If it meant having Sherry sprawled out on her bed, completely naked aside from a thin towel spread over her behind more often, then Lucy was all for it…

Lucy bit her lip as she stared down at Sherry. Her pale skin was shiny from the massage oil that Lucy had rubbed all over her before officially getting started with her massage, and her ass cheeks were poking out from underneath the tiny towel.

Lucy tried her best not to ogle Sherry's body, clearing her throat as she grabbed the bottle of oil and poured some more into the palm of her hand.

"I'm just gonna…" She drifted off, awkwardly straddling Sherry's behind before beginning to rub her neck and shoulders again.

"Shit," Sherry moaned as soon as Lucy's fingers came in contact with her skin again, and Lucy swallowed thickly, mentally scolding herself for the way her body reacted to the sound. Her hole clenched without her permission, her panties growing damp as she listened to her friend's satisfied moans.

As she worked her way down Sherry's back, Sherry's moans only grew even louder, breathier, needier. Lucy had given enough massages to be able to do it without having to pay much attention, so she allowed her mind to drift elsewhere as she continued kneading Sherry's flesh, but that was the worst thing that she could have possibly done.

Filthy images flashed through her mind as she wondered what else could make Sherry moan that way. She pictured Sherry lying among a pile of soft, fluffy pillows and blankets, blue eyes rolled into the back of her head as Lucy played with her breasts, fondling them, pinching and pulling on her nipples, sucking hickeys onto the plump flesh.

She pictured herself and Sherry lying side by side, facing each other, limbs tangled together as they stuck to each other like glue. Sweaty skin rubbing together as they exchanged a sloppy kiss and rolled their hips in a steady rhythm, cunts bumping against each other with every movement.

She pictured Sherry on top of her, sitting on her face, riding her tongue with her head thrown back, mouth wide open and hands cupping her breasts as she moaned so loudly that Lucy's neighbors would be able to hear it.

Lucy let out a quiet moan too, and then a gasp as she realized that she'd started moving, rolling her hips back and forth as she tried to grind her cunt against Sherry's behind.

Her cheeks felt as if they were on fire as she held her breath, staring at the back of Sherry's head, trying to figure out whether she'd noticed or not. It didn't seem that she had because she was still moaning, still whimpering, still mumbling about how good Lucy was.

Lucy could hardly breathe as she slowly moved back, straddling Sherry's legs in order to focus on Sherry's thighs instead. She hesitated for only a moment before her fingers dug into the tender flesh.

Lucy was practically drooling as she rubbed the back of Sherry's thigh, the smooth skin warming quickly under her touch. She tried to distract herself by looking around her bedroom rather than staring directly at Sherry's perfect skin, but there wasn't a hope that she could get her mind out of the gutter now. Every time she closed her eyes, all she could see was Sherry in one vulgar position or another, moaning and convulsing as she reached her completion.

Lucy's fingers traveled from the back of Sherry's thigh to the inside of it, and Sherry gasped, tensing up as Lucy's fingers disappeared underneath her towel, between her legs, and dangerously close to her cunt.

"Sorry!" Lucy apologized quickly, but Sherry merely lifted her behind, wiggling it from side to side for a moment before turning to look back at Lucy.

"No, you're fine, I'm just a little sensitive there," she giggled. "You can continue, but, ugh...If your fingers are gonna be so close to my cunt, then this massage better have a happy ending." She winked.

Lucy's eyes widened, and her mouth fell open as she choked out a surprised laugh and tried to figure out how to respond. She knew that Sherry was probably just joking around, but she also had the urge to scream at the top of her lungs, "Yes! Please let me give you a happy ending!"

Instead, she opened and closed her mouth like a fish, nodding before shaking her head before nodding again.

Sherry watched Lucy's glitching with an amused smile and a mischievous look in her eyes. "If I didn't know any better, Lucy, I'd say that you want me."

Only a blind fool could be oblivious to Lucy's constant staring, the way her fingers roamed a little too much, the way she stuttered and blushed whenever Sherry did or said...Well, anything. Sherry was well-aware of her friend's attraction to her. She was hoping that Lucy would finally act on it today, but clearly, she was going to need a little push.

"I-I—What do you mean?" Lucy forced out a laugh. "I don't want you, I...I don't want you!" she repeated as if that would somehow make it more convincing.

Sherry turned to lie on her back, propping herself up on her elbows, completely unbothered by the fact that she was left uncovered as the towel fell to her side. "Oh?" She quirked a perfectly arched brow as she tilted her head, a small pout forming on her lips. "You don't want me?"

"I—Well," Lucy let out another awkward laugh as she tried to figure out what to say. "That's not... Well, it's not like—"

"I want you," Sherry admitted easily, smiling when Lucy's eyes nearly bulged out of her head. "I want you to touch me. To kiss me. Make me feel good...And I want to do the same for you. You don't want that?"

Lucy was stunned into silence. Why wouldn't she? This was literally one of her wet dreams come to life! How many times had she sat around, daydreaming about what it would be like to have Sherry say those exact words to her? And now it was actually happening? Lucy wondered if she was just hallucinating.

Sherry giggled at the dumbstruck look on Lucy's face before yanking on the girl's shirt to pull her closer, and Lucy gasped as she was suddenly hovering over Sherry, their breasts rubbing together, only separated by the fabric of Lucy's crop top.

Sherry tugged at the hem of it as she stared into Lucy's pretty, round eyes. "Take this off."

Lucy had never followed orders so quickly before in her entire life. She pulled the shirt over her head, exposing her bare breasts, and she tried not to feel self-conscious as Sherry stared at her unabashedly.

"They're—smaller than yours," Lucy stuttered out in an attempt to point out her insecurity before Sherry could, but she only ended up feeling even more stupid for pointing out the obvious. "Sorry. I mean, not for the size of my boobs. I mean—"

"I like them," Sherry giggled and licked her lip as she brought a hand up to grope Lucy's breast. Lucy's breath hitched as her body tensed up, a shiver traveling down her spine. Sherry grinned, staring up at her with half-lidded eyes. "So cute. Are you a virgin?"

"What? No." Lucy blushed. "I've been with another girl before..." Although it was a long time ago, and Lucy had barely managed to cum.

"Mm," Sherry hummed before sitting up. Lucy gasped as Sherry maneuvered them with ease, and suddenly, Lucy was the one on her back, staring up at Sherry as Sherry hovered over her. "Mind if I take these off?" Sherry asked, and it took a few moments for the words to register, but Lucy quickly nodded when she realized that Sherry was tugging at her shorts.

"Yeah–No? No, I don't mind!"

The giggle that Sherry let out as she tugged down Lucy's shorts didn't make it any easier for Lucy to fight off her permanent blush. That, Lucy realized, was the fond little giggle that Sherry let out every time Lucy did something that she thought was cute. And the thought of Sherry finding her cute had Lucy's stomach knotting up, butterflies fluttering all around inside it.

"Wow." Sherry's sultry voice pulled Lucy out of her lovestruck thoughts and back into the moment. "No bra and no panties? Someone came prepared." She smirked. "Did you, by any chance, plan this?"

"No!" Lucy shook her head. She never in a million years could have anticipated that this would be happening, but she sure was glad that she'd chosen to wear the bare minimum anyway.

"Oh? So then you're just a little slut who likes to walk around with no underwear on?" Sherry smirked, an amused gleam in her eye as Lucy's widened. Lucy had to fight back an audible moan and the urge to beg Sherry to call her a slut again. Instead, she simply nodded, trying to keep her cool.

"Yeah, I guess I am. But let's not forget what you showed up wearing."

Nothing but a thin, silk robe that Lucy couldn't believe she felt comfortable leaving the house in.

Sherry let out a surprised laugh at Lucy's teasing. "Well, well, well. Look who finally grew some balls. What, are you done behaving like a shy little school-girl with a big, fat crush?"

Lucy crinkled her nose. "Don't bring up balls when we're about to have sex. Are you trying to ruin the mood?"

Sherry rolled her eyes and let out a giggle before leaning down to give Lucy a kiss. It was a quick peck, at first, but Lucy surprised her yet again by pulling her down and taking her mouth in a long and heated kiss.

Lucy licked Sherry's bottom lip before pushing her tongue between the girl's plump, pink lips, and Sherry opened up easily, groaning when Lucy's tongue slid over hers. Sherry tilted her head to deepen the kiss and tangled her tongue with Lucy's, letting out a squeak of surprise when Lucy pulled away and bit down on her bottom lip before sucking on it gently.

The two of them became lost in the sloppy kiss, growing increasingly desperate the longer it continued. Lucy moaned into Sherry's mouth as Sherry began playing with her breasts, pinching one of her nipples while gently rubbing a thumb over the other. Meanwhile, Lucy's hands were roaming Sherry's body, sliding over each and every one of her curves, digging into her soft skin.

Sherry pulled away from their kiss and began pressing open-mouthed kisses along Lucy's jawline, all over Lucy's neck, and down to her breasts, where Sherry placed all her focus.

"Shit," Lucy murmured, lazily running her fingers through Sherry's hair as Sherry sucked one of her nipples into her mouth. "I'm sensitive t-there," she moaned, squirming as she squeezed her eyes shut.

"I bet you're sensitive here too," Sherry commented before pushing two fingers between the folds of Lucy's cunt. Lucy gasped as Sherry slid her fingers up and down her center a few times before rubbing them over her clit.

Sherry leaned up to kiss Lucy again as she gave the girl's clit a pinch that had her flinching and letting out a breathy moan. When Sherry's fingers traveled down, the tips of them poking at Lucy's entrance, Lucy quickly pulled away from their kiss again.

"I can't–I won't last long if you..."

"Isn't that the whole point?" Sherry smirked. "I want to make you cum all over my fingers."

Before Lucy could say anything, Sherry leaned down to give her another extended kiss before pulling away and repositioning herself again. She turned her back to Lucy before straddling her stomach, then wiggled her hips as she looked back at Lucy. "I want you to eat me out. Okay?"

"Fuck, yes," Lucy groaned as she grabbed Sherry's sides, pulling her back a little. She didn't waste any time before pushing Sherry's cheeks apart and pushing her tongue between the lips of the girl's cunt.

Sherry sucked in a sharp breath as Lucy's tongue began exploring her pussy, flicking over her clit a few times before swirling around her entrance and then poking inside of it. Sherry just about melted into a puddle right then and there, her arms giving out on her as she pressed her torso against Lucy's stomach.

It took a couple of seconds for her to pull herself together enough to focus on making Lucy feel good too, but when she finally did, she spread the lips of Lucy's cunt apart with two fingers, immediately swirling her tongue around the girl's clit before beginning to suck on it. She slowly pushed her middle finger inside of Lucy's hole, groaning as she felt the way Lucy twitched and spasmed around her.

Sherry replaced her one finger with two and started up a steady pace, thrusting them in and out of Lucy's cunt quickly as she allowed her spit to dribble off her tongue and between Lucy's folds. Lucy was already dripping wet with her own slick, the wet sound of Sherry's fingers plunging in and out of her filling the room along with their moans.

Sherry used her other hand to hold Lucy's hips down as they bucked up, the girl's thighs quivering as she pushed herself against Sherry's fingers, meeting her thrusts. Sherry could tell that she was already getting close by the way her moans were getting louder and her tongue moved irregularly, losing its rhythm.

Still, Sherry could barely keep herself together as Lucy's tongue worked its magic. Lucy lapped Sherry's wetness up greedily, nibbling on the sensitive skin around her cunt, spitting into Sherry's hole before slurping the mess right back out. She had to keep her arms wrapped around Sherry's thighs to keep the girl from running away from the intense pleasure, and she was determined to make Sherry cum on her tongue. She wanted to taste even more of her, and she could tell that she was getting closer.

"Fuck," Sherry slurred, pushing herself back against Lucy's tongue as she began rubbing quick circles around Lucy's clit. Lucy gasped, the pit of her stomach burning hot with pleasure that was threatening to spill over at any moment. "Yes, just like that, baby. Feels so good–just like that!" Sherry's eyes rolled into the back of her head as she continued fucking herself back onto Lucy's tongue, biting her lip to keep herself from getting too loud. Not that it helped much. When Lucy began sucking on her clit again, her whole body tensed up before suddenly, waves of pleasure were crashing over her, and her orgasm was bursting out of her. She came with a loud shout, gasping for breath as Lucy held her in place and continued eating her out even as the pleasure started to become overwhelming.

Lucy wasn't far behind. Sherry could feel the girl clenching and unclenching around her fingers as she continued pounding into her, crooking her fingers until they hit the small bundle of nerves inside of her. Lucy let out a string of curses and loud moans of her own as her back arched off the bed and her legs snapped shut, only for Sherry to push them apart once again before continuing to finger her.

Lucy was seeing stars, and Sherry was seeing nothing but blur as the two of them fucked each other through their orgasms. They were both nothing more than a pile of sweaty skin and bones that felt more like jelly as they tried to come down from their high. Sherry managed to roll off of Lucy and reposition herself so that she was lying beside her. Lucy let out some sort of tired noise–a mix of a delighted laugh, a tired groan, and a satisfied moan– as she rolled over until she was lying half on top of Sherry and half on the bed.

Sherry grunted as Lucy kneed her in the side while attempting to wrap a leg around her, but aside from that, neither of them said or did anything aside from trying to catch their breath.

Until a few minutes later, when Lucy was mostly conscious of the world around her again and had enough strength to lift her head and look at Sherry.

"Well, that was fucking amazing!" She paused for a few moments before sending Sherry a hopeful look. "We're gonna have a round two, right?"

A lazy grin made its way onto Sherry's face as

she attempted to nod, but she was still too tired to do such a strenuous activity. It had been a long time since she'd cum that hard. Still, there was only one right answer to the question.

"Obviously."

He Likes To Watch

By Victoria Jimenez

"Come on in." Carmen smiled as she opened the front door to let Carlos in. "I'm glad you're here! I've been horny all day, and it's about time someone did something about it..." Her dark eyes trailed over to look at the man sitting on the living room couch, and her gaze turned cold as she let out a quiet sigh. "Just ignore my husband, Ray. He's not man enough for me, so you're going to fuck me while he watches. Maybe he'll pick up some tips."

The man all but whined as Carlos chuckled and looked him up and down before turning to Carmen again. "No problem. Do you want it on the couch, or would you prefer it if I fucked you right in the middle of you and your husband's bed?"

Carmen bit her lip and pressed her thighs

together as she stared up at the smug-looking man. She could hardly stand to wait any longer, and honestly, she didn't care if he decided to take her right in the middle of the living room floor, on the couch, against the wall, whatever—but then again, her getting fucked by another man in their bed would be far more humiliating for Ray.

So with a large smirk on her face, she wordlessly grabbed Carlos' hand and turned to lead him toward the bedroom. She didn't even need to look in order to know that Ray was scurrying behind them like a lost puppy. He just barely managed to make it into the room before they slammed the door shut in his face.

"Okay, let's get straight to it. I want it doggy style," Carmen said as she unhooked her bra and shimmied out of her underwear before climbing onto the bed. "Ray can never last for more than a minute when we do doggy style." She rolled her eyes.

"I'm not surprised," Carlos murmured as he positioned himself behind Carmen, grabbing her hips to pull her toward him and pushing her down until her back was arched. She looked picture perfect in this position.

Carlos took a few moments to explore her body, tugging at the long, dark brown hair that cascaded down her back, running his hands along her smooth, golden skin, and kneading the meaty flesh of her large behind between his fingertips. He sucked in a breath when he pushed her cheeks apart to get a better look at her cunt and saw that she was already dripping wet.

"A man like that can't handle a woman like you," he continued as he allowed his middle finger to run between her folds. Carmen shivered, twitching a little as he briefly poked the tip of his finger inside her hole before pulling it away again. "How did he even manage to convince you to settle for him?"

"I thought he was a real man," she grumbled under her breath. "He was handsome, tall, strong-looking, all muscles. He had a voice so deep that it made me want to drop my panties right on the spot—and most of all, he had the biggest cock that I'd ever seen in my life..." She sighed and shook her head as she turned to look at him.

Unsurprisingly, Ray was in the midst of slowly stroking himself, already a little red in the face, chest already heaving as his dark eyes watched the two of them closely. He bit down on his plump lower lip, thumb sliding over the slit of his cock. He didn't even pretend to not be turned on by the sight of his own wife on all fours for some other man.

Carmen rolled her eyes. "It's such a damn

shame. Such a waste for him to be gifted with such an impressive cock when he doesn't even know how to use the damn thing properly!" she scoffed, and Ray let out a low noise, something along the lines of a whine or a whimper, or some other unmanly sound that caused her to roll her eyes again before turning to face away from him. "He's so pathetic, I swear… Carlos, why don't you go ahead and show him how a real man does it, hm? I don't need any prep. Just get inside me!"

Carlos was unfazed by her orders, simply grabbing the back of her neck and shoving her face into the pillows once she'd turned to glare at him after a few seconds had gone by without him doing what she'd told him to.

"Well, for starters, a real man doesn't take orders from mouthy little brats with bad attitudes like you," he chuckled. "Believe me, I'll fuck you when I'm good and ready. Just be quiet and stay still for me until then, hm?" he mocked.

Carmen lifted her head, turning to send him another glare, but she didn't open her mouth to say anything else, so he ignored it, smirking as he plunged two fingers inside of her, crooking them for a moment before pulling them out. The hard look melted off of Carmen's face in an instant, her eyes widening a little and her lips parting as she sucked in a quiet breath.

"So wet," he commented, pausing for a moment to suck on the two fingers that had just been inside her. He let out a satisfied hum before pulling them out of his mouth and burying them inside of her cunt again. "You really weren't lying about being horny all day, huh?"

Carmen was a little too preoccupied with rocking herself back against his fingers to answer. Two fingers really weren't enough to clench her craving—she'd been fantasizing about being filled to the brim with cock all day, just dying to finally experience the wonderful feeling of being stretched and full again—but it was something, which was better than nothing. She could feel the tips of his fingers just barely grazing the soft spot inside of her every time she pushed herself back, and she closed her eyes, her brows furrowing as she put all of her focus on that feeling.

"And you have the audacity to call your husband pathetic," Carlos snickered. "You're the one acting like a bitch in heat."

"Maybe I wouldn't be so desperate if my good-for-nothing husband took care of my needs!" she spat, her accent becoming thicker as her words slurred together. Carlos glanced over at Ray, scoffing as he caught sight of the man pouting with his hand wrapped around his cock.

"Can't argue with that." He narrowed his eyes at Ray before turning to look at Carmen again. She let out a loud whine when he removed his fingers, and then a surprised squeal when he pinched her clit harshly between his thumb and forefinger. "You want me to fuck you, Carmen?"

"Isn't that what I've been telling you this whole time?!" she growled.

"Yes, but you haven't asked. Ask me to fuck you. Beg me to fuck you."

"I've never had to beg a man for anything in my whole life, especially not to fuck me."

"There's a first time for everything."

"I'm not going to beg you–"

"That's fine. I can just go back home and call up some other desperate slut who'll be just as eager for me to fuck her, and you can stay here with your pathetic excuse for a husband and enjoy the fifteen seconds of sex that he'll be able to give you before he blows his load and calls it a night. Your choice."

Carmen stared at Carlos with the most venomous expression that she could muster up, and Carlos simply quirked a brow at her, his lips pulling up into his usual smirk as he moved to get off the bed only to have her reach back to grab his wrist.

"Please," she gritted out. "Fuck me."

"You can do better than that, sweetheart. Where's your enthusiasm?"

"Carlos—" She heaved a heavy sigh as she sent him her best set of puppy dog eyes. A stark contrast to her previous death glare. "I want it more than anything. I want you to fuck me, okay? Please? Will you please fuck me?"

"Good job asking for what you want." He smiled. "Now beg like I told you to."

"That was me begging!" she whined, slapping the mattress in frustration as if that would do anything aside from making the smug expression on Carlos' face become even more unbearable.

"Not quite. Try it again. Or you can let Ray–"

"Please just fuck me already!" she cried. "I just want to feel full and–and I want you to fuck me until I can't even think anymore, and I want you to show Ray what it looks like to pleasure a woman properly, and I want to cum! I want you to make me cum, and I want you to cum inside me too and–"

"No!" Ray suddenly called from the couch, eyes as wide as saucers as the two of them turned to look at him. Carlos rolled his eyes at the man before letting out a cruel laugh.

"What's the matter, Ray? You don't want another man coming inside your wife?"

"No..." he practically whispered as he stared between the two of them.

"Maybe you should have thought about that before she called me over." Carlos shrugged. Ray watched with a helpless expression on his face as Carlos grabbed Carmen's sides, pushing her down until her back was arched even more, her ass lifted high up in the air, ready and waiting.

He wrapped a hand around the base of his cock, rubbing the tip of it between Carmen's folds a few times before sinking inside of her with one swift thrust. Carmen gasped and choked on her own spit as she was caught off guard. One second she'd been clenching around nothing, wiggling her ass in the air as she waited for an intrusion that she was starting to think would never come, and the next, Carlos' balls were slapping against her cunt as he breached her, his cock resting hard and heavy inside of her, dragging against her inner walls as he pulled out before slamming back in again.

Carlos gave a couple of hard thrusts just to hear the sound of his skin slapping against hers as she let out strained cries, moans of pleasure mixed with whimpers of pain and words of thanks slurred together as she finally got what she wanted from him.

It was only a couple of seconds later when he picked up the pace and stuck to a steady rhythm, beginning to pound into her with harsh thrusts that caused the whole bed to rock, the headboard crashing into the wall and Carmen clinging to the sheets in an attempt to keep herself steady.

"There we go." Carlos let out a breathless chuckle, his eyes glued to Carmen's ass as it smacked against his hips repeatedly. "You're finally getting what you wanted, now what should you say?"

"Tha–Thank y-you," she stammered, sucking in a sharp breath when Carlos grabbed her hair, winding it around his fist for a better grip as he forced her upper body up off the bed. He turned her head until she was facing Ray, and she couldn't help but moan as she caught sight of him frowning with his hand wrapped around the base of his angry-red cock, clearly trying to keep himself from coming prematurely.

"Jesus." She let out a breathy laugh, trying to keep her eyes on him even as they threatened to slip shut. "I've never seen a sadder sight in my entire life. How could you be sitting there playing with your big, dumb, useless cock while another man takes care of your wife in your own bed? Don't you have any f-fucking shame?"

She paused and bit her lip, trying to find the strength to speak again, but it took her a while to find her voice as Carlos tugged harder on her hair, slapping her ass with his free hand before pushing down on her lower back again. She was starting to see stars dancing around in her vision as he split her open on his cock, her cunt throbbing and pulsating enough to distract her from berating her husband for a short time.

Everything faded away for a moment as she melted into the mattress, focusing on nothing aside from the feeling of the big, strong man on top of her forcing his cock in and out of her at a rapid speed. By the time she remembered what she was supposed to be doing—throwing insults at her spineless husband—she was drooling.

Even drooling and stuttering and shaking like a leaf as Carlos drew his hand back and spanked her several more times until his handprint was visible on her skin, she was still somehow less pitiful than Ray.

"H-How does it feel to—ah—" She sucked in a sharp breath as Carlos changed his position slightly, angling his hips in order to fuck her even deeper.

Now he was slamming right into her G-spot with every thrust, and Carmen could feel her pussy twitching and her skin heating up and stomach tingling as she got closer to her orgasm. "—to see a real man fucking your w-wife and doing what you never could?" she finished, giggling as she watched Ray's expression morph into one of a kicked puppy.

"You think you sitting there looking sad is going to make me feel bad for you? No, I feel bad for me. This is how I deserve to be fucked all the time, but instead, I have to put up with you and your deplorable little cock! You're so fucking hopeless, Ray, I swear! So pointless for you to have such a nice cock and no skills to use it–Shit!" she gasped when Carlos let go of her hair, her face suddenly buried in the sheets beneath her. She tried to lift her head, but Carlos' hand was pressed against the back of it, effectively holding her down.

"Sorry, sweetheart, nothing personal. It's just that I'm never gonna be able to cum if I have to keep listening to you go on and on about your husband's so-called 'cock,'" he grunted. "I'll let you sit up again if you can keep that big mouth of yours shut, though. Think you can do that?"

She groaned a short slew of indecipherable words, and Carlos took that as a yes, grabbing her hair and lifting her head again before pulling her in for a rough kiss. The angle was awkward, uncomfortable, and borderline painful for Carmen, who had to strain her neck in order to meet his lips, but that and the way Carlos grabbed her breast with his other hand before sliding it down to clutch her stomach only added to her pleasure. She felt dirty and thoroughly used, and there was no better feeling on Earth, in her opinion.

"You fuck me so good," she moaned once he pulled away from her lips. "So good, Papi, so good, so good–"

"Shit," Carlos groaned as he felt her pussy spasming around his cock, slipping out of her for a moment as her wetness made things a little more slippery, but he quickly pushed himself inside of her again, drilling into her with newfound determination as he chased his own orgasm.

Carmen screamed as he slammed in and out of her repeatedly, holding her down and making her take the brutal pounding even as she tried to squirm away from the overwhelming feeling of pleasure. Eventually, she gave up, her body becoming pliant underneath his as her mind drifted off to God knew where. She was barely conscious as she drooled and cried and screamed and moaned until her vocal cords were sore. She couldn't make out the filthy words that Carlos was murmuring in her ear, barely even registered him wrapping his hand around her neck and squeezing until she struggled to take a full breath. But the unmistakable feeling of him pulling out of her brought her back to reality with a sudden jolt.

She whined, squirming around just slightly, wiggling her ass as if to entice him to fill her up with his cock again, but it didn't work. Carlos groaned, throwing his head back as he stroked himself quickly. Despite what he'd said earlier, he knew that coming inside of her wasn't an option, but covering her plump ass with his seed instead was just fine with him.

All it took was him looking down between them and catching sight of her sopping wet cunt, thoroughly fucked open and still convulsing as her wetness leaked out of her and onto the sheets, and suddenly, he was shooting his load all over her ass with a low groan.

Carmen let out a quiet moan as she felt his cum landing over the globes of her ass, some dripping onto her pussy, between her lips, making her feel even filthier than she already had before. Her cunt throbbed as she turned and watched Carlos wordlessly climb off the bed and head to the bathroom once he was finished. It was as if he'd gotten what he'd wanted and now he was done with her. The thought made her feel low, used, and horny all over again as a result, but she ignored the heartbeat between her legs and let out a soft moan as she turned over to lie on her back instead, then turned her head to look at Ray, who was already standing up and walking over.

He wordlessly climbed on top of her, stroking his cock as he stared down at her heaving chest, her big breasts on full display and looking just as perfect as they always did. He groaned as he came all over her tits, his cum splattering over her nipples and the soft flesh of her breasts until he had no more of his seed left to give.

By the time he was finished, he was breathless and trembling from the intensity of his orgasm, struggling to hold himself upright as he threw his head back.

"Fuck," he murmured when he'd finally managed to breathe again. "Thank you, baby."

"You're welcome," Carmen giggled, suddenly sounding like her usual, shy self. "Happy birthday!"

"Happy birthday to me," Ray chuckled before leaning down to press a gentle kiss to her lips.

Mistress

My Amanda Moss

The bed beside Richard was cold when he woke, and in his sleepy state, he glanced around for his wife. There was no sight of her in the room, and he experienced a sudden jolt of excitement when he tried to move his hands. They were each tied to a bedpost, he realized, and he was completely naked.

He heard footsteps coming up the hallway stairs. Seconds later, his bedroom door swung open, and Tara stood in the doorway. Just the sight of her took his breath away, as it always did. She wore a black leather corset that covered her torso and pushed her breasts up so they were almost spilling over, and her pussy was completely exposed. Black boots were laced up to her knees, with a sexy heel that clicked with every step.

Richard loved his wife. She was a spectacular woman, and she was the perfect housewife. He never had to request anything from her; it was almost as if she could read his mind. The two of them flowed together flawlessly, and he couldn't imagine being with anyone else.

Richard worked long hours during the week as the CEO of a large investment company. Every day, he managed hundreds of people and their duties, and it was tiresome. He had every weekend off, and to take a break from his normal routine, he let Tara take control of him and boss him around. It was quite fun.

His wife, though innocent during the week, was quite the dominatrix. During the weekends, she was his Mistress, and she made damn sure he knew it.

She tilted her head to the side, glancing him over with a disapproving look. "Do you think you can just lie around all day?" she crooned, slowly strutting toward him. His eyes followed her as she approached his side of the bed, swinging her leg over and straddling his lap. *God, she's so sexy*, he thought, admiring her body as she stared down at him. *I'm one lucky man.* "Don't you know that there's work to be done?" She gave him a sharp slap across his face, and he did his best not to wince. "I asked you a question, Richard."

"Yes, Mistress, I know there's work to be done," he responded quickly, more awake after the slap. She was the dominatrix, he was her submissive; in his half-asleep state, that hadn't fully registered.

He gazed up at her as she shifted her body forward so that she hovered over his face. He had the perfect view of her beautiful, juicy pussy. "Are you ready to get to work?" she demanded.

"I'm ready, Mistress." He could taste her already and was ready to do her bidding.

Tara straddled his face, moving her pussy dangerously close to his mouth. His mouth began to water for her. "I bet you are. Now get started."

She lowered herself onto his face, applying force, and he was greeted with the familiar feeling of her wet pussy and tight ass against his face and tongue.

His tongue mixed back and forth around her clit, and she sighed. "Oh, you're so good. You're such a good boy. Lick my clit harder." He did as she commanded, rewarded with a soft moan. "Good boy. Move your tongue in circles."

He lapped up every drop of her sweet nectar, inhaling her intoxicating scent. Anything for his Mistress. Her breathing was coming faster and faster, and he longed to be able to touch her with his hands. He itched to run his fingers along her breasts, to tease and pluck at her nipples until she screamed, but today she was in control.

"Harder, harder!" she demanded, crying out. Her entire body spasmed above him, so hard he could feel the trembling in her pussy. "Don't stop!" She rode his face for a few more moments before lightly lifting himself up, freeing his lips.

She steadied herself against the wall for a moment, breathing heavily, before staring down at Richard once more. She leaned down, her hair brushing his face and tickling. He shivered at the sensation, eager to please her more.

Tara whispered in his ear. "That was... mmm, so good." A shiver wracked his whole body as her breath tingled against his skin, and his cock rose just a little more. "You're such a good boy." She laughed as she pulled his head up by his hair, gripping tightly. "Tell me how good of a boy you are."

"I'm a good boy, Mistress," he responded rapidly, desperate for more abuse. He loved it just as much as she did.

She opened her legs once again, and as she reached down to rub her clit, she took him by surprise and started rubbing herself on his face. He groaned with pleasure as his mouth was suddenly filled with her pussy once more. He continued to lick and suck at her delicate pussy lips; he couldn't get enough.

"Eat me out until I cum," she told him, and he was more than willing. "Tell me what you're going to do."

"I'm going to eat you out until you cum," he mumbled through her pussy lips, tongue-fucking her.

He had never felt so hungry for her before, he was desperate to please her. His lips and tongue were burning with her taste, so delicious. He sucked and licked her pussy, flicking his tongue back and forth across her clit.

Her fingers gripped the back of his head, her thighs squeezing his head tightly as she panted above him.

His cock was hard and pressing against his underwear. His balls felt swollen, and they ached with the need to release, but only with her permission. He could only hope she would give it to him soon.

Tara began to moan. Her moans came faster and faster until she was breathing in short, ragged breaths. His tongue was growing sore moving back and forth inside her pussy, but he was determined to do as she demanded.

Her hips bucked against his head as she came

hard, gasping. "Oh fuck, oh fuck," she moaned. "God, you have suck a talented fucking mouth."

He kissed the inside of her thighs as she caught her breath again, loving the feel of her soft skin. "Kissing me is not going to bring you better treatment," Tara told him. She slid off his body and leaned over him, undoing the binding around his wrists. "Stand up," she commanded, stepping back. He hurried to do as she told him, and she beckoned for him to follow him with her finger. He followed closely behind her, keeping his eyes on her sweet, exposed ass.

She led him into their spare bedroom, shoving him inside and slamming the door shut behind them. It was a room they only used on the weekends, when Tara was having her way. It was their BDSM dungeon; within, they had muzzles, rope, collars, wrist and ankle restraints, and a large, soft bed fitted with velvet sheets. Just the sight of it made his cock rise all the way up, and he curiously wondered what his Mistress was going to do to him today.

"Get on the bed," she ordered him, smacking his ass to get him to move faster. As he climbed on, she shoved him again so that he was on his back. Above him, suspended from the ceiling, was a spreader bar. It hadn't been there the previous weekend, so she must have just purchased it. Tara did love her toys, and she had a credit card solely for the purpose of her purchasing whatever she wanted.

"Lift your legs up." He did so, watching excitedly as his wife secured his ankles to either side of the spreader bar. He was utterly exposed, and the thought of it made it the hairs on his arm stand on end. She turned away from him for only a moment, grinning wickedly when she returned and presented two pairs of handcuffs. "Hold out your hands."

He winced as she tightly secured each of his hands to different bedposts, gulping with anticipation as she dragged her hand down his chest. He was so hard, his erection glaringly obvious, and she laughed at him. "I'm sorry, is this making you horny?" she teased, slapping his cock lightly with the palm of her hand. The feel of her skin on his delicate member only intensified his desire for her.

"Yes, Mistress. You make me horny," he told her honestly.

"Flattery will get you nowhere. You're not allowed to cum yet, Richard. Not until I've had my way." She walked over to the wall, exaggerating the sway of her hips, and paused in front of her sizable collection of cock rings. "My, my, my. Which one should we play with?" She delicately dragged her hand along each one, glancing over at Richard with a sly look. "Why don't you choose?"

Somehow, he knew this was a trick. No matter which cock ring he chose, she was going to select the one she wanted to use. She likely already had one in mind. His eyes scanned over them, landing on a simple one. It was fitted with loops so that its size could be adjusted. "That one, Mistress," he stated, nodding his head toward it.

She followed his gaze and laughed. "You would choose that one, wouldn't you? You're a pussy, Richard. I want to hear you say it."

"I'm a pussy, Mistress," he said obediently.

"No, I have something a little more... adventurous in mind." She reached for the highest one on the wall, and his gaze once more went to her delicious ass.

The ring she chose had a connecting chain with clamps connected to it, which were meant for his nipples. She walked over to him and slowly, delicately, slid the ring onto him. She lightly traced her index finger up and down his shaft, gauging his reaction as she deliberately licked her full lips. "My, you're quite large. Do you want me?"

"Yes, Mistress." He wanted her so fucking badly

that his body was trembling. He craved more of her touch.

"Do you want to fuck me?"

"Yes, Mistress."

"Louder!" she shouted, grabbing hold of his cock and squeezing. His body jerked at the sudden pressure, and the touch alone almost made him cum.

"Yes, Mistress!" he screamed.

"That's too bad, because that's not what's going to happen next." He winced as she connected each clamp to one of his nipples, making sure they were secured tightly.

His heartbeat picked up when she grabbed hold of her flogger, lightly twirling it around. Out of her paddles and whips, she enjoyed using the flogger the most, and Richard enjoyed it as well. It brought him both pain and pleasure. "Because you've been naughty, haven't you?"

"Yes, Mistress," he breathed.

She stood before him, holding the flogger in her right hand. Gently, she dragged it along his cock, and his eyes almost rolled into the back of his head at how amazing the leather felt on his skin. "Say it louder."

"Yes, Mistress."

He gasped when she stepped back and smacked his bare ass with the flogger. It stung, and one of the strands clipped the edge of his ball sack. She shook her head in disappointment, clicking her tongue. "Dear me, it seems I didn't do it hard enough. You barely made any noise."

She flogged him again, and he grunted with pain. "Did I hit you hard enough, Richard?"

"Yes, Mistress."

She hit him harder, and he cried out as his lust grew. "I think you're lying, Richard. Am I hitting you hard enough, Richard?"

"No, Mistress."

"Should I hit you harder then?"

"Yes, Mistress." *Fuck yes.*

She swatted him again and again, each time harder than the last. "Will you lie to me again?"

"No, Mistress," he whimpered. Richard grunted with both pain and pleasure as his wife spanked him once more. He loved for her to take control. She lifted her arms, giving him freedom to lift his backside high, ready for her to strike again and proving his eagerness. She grinned unexpectedly but tried to hide it. He sighed, moaning as his wife's palm connected with his cheek instead of the flogger.

"God, you're so hard," she commented, amused. She swiped his tip with her finger, gazing down curiously at the droplet of cum on her finger. Slowly, she licked it off, and more of his juices leaked out in response. "You want to cum, don't you?"

"Yes, Mistress," he all but begged.

"Oh, I know you do. Don't worry, it's almost time." Her smile was mischievous as she pulled a metal wand from behind her back. He wanted to frown. He hadn't noticed her grab it, but he should have known; it was one of her favorite toys.

He moaned as she slipped the wand into his ass, jumping at how cold it was and internally amazed at how easily it entered him. It was ribbed, and he felt each rib as it entered his anal cavity. She slid it slowly in and out, and he felt his cock throb at the stimulation. "Do you like that?" she whispered, crouching down so that he could no longer see her. Her breath tickled his crotch. "Do you like feeling like there's a cock in your ass?"

"Yes, Mistress!"

It was unnerving, having her mouth that close to his crotch. He was desperate for release; his cock was throbbing so hard it was almost painful. She slid the wand farther in, chuckling lightly.

"I think you've been punished enough, you bad boy. You took it well." She lowered her voice. "Do you think you deserve a reward?"

"Yes!" he moaned as she began to lightly stroke his shaft.

She tightened her grip on him. "Yes what?"

"Yes, Mistress!"

Oh, God. She continued to run her hand up and down his cock, and he was well aware of how much she was enjoying herself. "Do you think you deserve to have my mouth on your cock?"

"Yes! Yes, Mistress!"

Richard lifted his head, watching his wife with amazement as she took his penis into her mouth and began to suck on it, her hands lovingly fondling his balls. She loved to play with his balls, but she had never given him such intimate attention while she was in dominatrix mode. Richard couldn't take his eyes off her as she played with him. He could feel himself about to climax any second, and he didn't want to miss a moment, though he tried to hold it in.

"No cumming until I say so," Tara warned him, her hands replacing her mouth on his genitals. "It's not time."

"I..."—Richard stopped to gasp for air—"...can't... hold...on...Mistress..." He felt himself going, a flood of pleasure threatening to overwhelm him. It wasn't enough to push him over, but it was close.

"No cumming, or I swear I will spank the shit out of you!"

With that, Tara continued sucking him to the edge and held him there. He could feel himself slipping away. He couldn't hold back his desire anymore. As her hands rubbed his cock, he felt himself tingle in her hands. As he envisioned her bouncing up and down on his cock, moaning, he felt another rush of lust and desire. He was about to burst; it was too intense.

"Richard, don't you dare come until I say so!" She licked up his shaft, licking his balls before wrapping her tongue around the tip.

"Oh fuck," he sighed, shifting his hips. "Please fuck me, Mistress."

"You want me to fuck you?" She smiled. "No need to beg me, darling." She began to suck him harder and faster, squeezing his cock in her mouth and licking him. She wanted his pleasure.

"Please fuck me, just like this. I want to feel my cock fill your pussy with cum, Mistress," he begged her.

She took his shaft and began stroking again. "Is that what you want? To fill me with your cum?" she asked, amused.

"Yes, please fuck me. Please don't stop." His balls

tightened, and his cock twitched, pleading for more of her attention.

In seconds, her outfit was off, thrown to the floor. Her perky breasts exposed, she straddled him, slipping his cock deep inside of her. He was delighted to feel how wet she was. She let out a soft moan as she settled herself. "The same rules apply," she said almost breathlessly. "You are not allowed to cum until I say so."

"Fuck, fuck," he cried as he clenched his legs in pleasure, her pussy gripping his cock. "Please Mistress, make me come," he pleaded as she rocked her hips.

"You cannot have your orgasm until I say it's time." She continued riding him, letting his cock sink into her pussy.

He knew if he came, he would be in big trouble, and she would punish him harshly. He loved the way his cock felt in her pussy, and he loved her to ride him, but he wasn't sure how much longer he could hold his orgasm in. She was going to do what she wanted until she was satisfied.

He loved the way she rode his cock. She leaned forward a bit, sliding her pussy down the length of him and winking. Her pussy was clenched so tightly around him that he almost came. He was having a hard time controlling himself. This was the most intense feeling of pure pleasure he had ever experienced.

She leaned forward again, and this time she was aiming her pussy downward as she rode him. She was riding him and squeezing him and fucking him with her pussy. He wished he could grip on to her hips or the headboard to steady himself, but the handcuffs held his hands firmly in place. She was bouncing on his cock faster and faster.

Tara began bucking and rubbing her pussy on him with force, her gasps coming faster and faster until she spasmed above him. The spasms in her pussy threw him overboard, and he screamed with her as white-hot pleasure shot through him, overwhelming his senses.

She shuddered again, relaxing down onto his cock and giving him a satisfied smile, her cheeks flushed. "I didn't tell you to cum, but you're forgiven. Good boy."

Who's The Boss
By Jordan W. Miller

Rob tapped his foot impatiently as he knocked on the door more times than what was necessary, until finally, he heard an annoyed shout. "Come in!"

He flung the door open and slammed it shut behind him, taking long strides over to the surprised-looking woman's desk until he was standing right in front of it, staring her down.

"Rob, what are you still doing here? It's 5 p.m. You were supposed to get off an hour ago, weren't you?"

"I'm here to turn in my letter of resignation," he told her before thrusting the paper onto her desk. "I no longer wish to work here."

The dark-skinned woman's brown eyes widened even more as she quickly skimmed the paper before looking up at him again. She shook her head, shooting out of her seat and practically running to the other side of her desk to stand in front of him.

"What? But this is so sudden! You're one of this company's best employees! You've been working here for the last four and a half years, and you were next in line for a huge promotion! You can't just up and quit like this—"

"Tracey, I don't give a damn about any of that, and you know I don't." Rob sent her a hard look as he took a step closer to her. "While I work here, you're my boss, and I'm your employee, and it's against company policy for us to have any sort of relationship outside of a strictly professional one. You know that."

"Yes, but—"

"So I quit," Rob cut her off. "I can find another stuffy office job anywhere, and a man with my credentials will have no problem finding work with some other hotshot company. But where the hell am I supposed to find another woman like you?"

"I..." Tracey let out an exasperated laugh, shaking her head at him. "This is...Really, are you sure you don't want to think about this a little more? Quitting your job just for the sake of being with me is crazy!"

"No, it's not," Rob chuckled. "Missing out on the opportunity to be with the woman I love because of some silly job is crazy. I need you way more than I need this job, do you understand?"

Tracey opened her mouth in an attempt to say something else, but nothing came out. It wasn't very often that she was left speechless, but Rob always seemed to be the cause when she was.

Rob took a few more moments to search Tracey's chocolate eyes, trying to gauge her reaction. It was clear that she was surprised, but he wasn't quite sure why. He would jump into the middle of ongoing traffic or fling himself off a bridge for her without a second thought if she asked him to, and he thought that much was obvious.

But maybe not. Maybe he hadn't made it clear how much he truly loved her. He'd never been good with words, and expressing his feelings freely was a foreign concept to him, but he could show her how he felt about her better than he could tell her.

He pulled her in for a heated kiss before he could even think to stop himself, groaning as she immediately reciprocated it. Tracey tilted her head to deepen the kiss, wrapping her arms around Rob's neck as he pressed the palm of his hand against her lower back to pull her closer, his other hand squeezing her hip as he maneuvered them until Tracey's back was to her desk.

He easily lifted her up, setting her on the desk and standing between her legs as he haphazardly moved things around to make room for them. Neither of them paid any attention to the papers and folders that went flying off the desk, landing in a mess on the floor that the two of them would dread having to reorganize later.

Tracey wrapped her legs around Rob's waist, running her fingers through his silky blond hair as he fumbled with the buttons on his pants.

"We shouldn't be doing this," Tracey murmured after pulling away from the kiss for a brief moment, though her words were useless as she leaned forward again, opening her mouth to allow his tongue to slip inside.

The building was nearly empty anyway, and Tracey's office was up on the top floor. If they were quick enough, they'd be able to finish without being interrupted by yet another helpless employee coming in to ask yet another question that they should already know the answer to.

"We can stop if you want to," Rob offered anyway upon breaking their kiss to pull Tracey's top over her head. Her locs fell over her shoulders as Rob flung the shirt to the side, and he gently pushed them behind her back before unhooking her bra with one hand.

Tracey didn't answer, instead focusing on pulling Rob's cock through the hole in his unbuttoned pants. She sucked in a quiet breath as it sprang out, already glistening wet with precum, the tip of it an angry red color.

Rob had been waiting desperately for the moment that he'd finally get to have her for months now, and no matter how many times he'd jerked off to the thought of her, he'd never been able to fully satisfy his needs. He felt as if he would lose his mind if he didn't get to have her soon, and Tracey felt the exact same way.

Her panties were soaked through, Rob discovered as soon as he'd pushed his hand up her skirt, cupping the mound of flesh between her legs. She spread her thighs farther apart, moaning into his mouth as he pushed her panties to the side and gave her clit a small pinch.

Her hips rolled on their own accord as she tried to grind against his hand, desperate for more friction, more relief, more pleasure. But Rob pulled his hand away before she could find a steady rhythm, and

Tracey let out a quiet whine as she was suddenly left with nothing.

"Fuck," Rob practically whispered after pushing two fingers into his mouth. "You taste so good." His eyes darkened as he stared into Tracey's, and Tracey's mouth fell open as he brought the hand down to wrap around his cock, stroking it a few times to get it nice and wet.

He hooked his arms underneath her thighs afterward, dragging her closer to the edge of the desk and lining himself up with her entrance quickly.

"Are you ready?" he asked in between planting kisses on her lips.

"Yes, yes, yes." She nodded quickly. "I want you inside me now!"

"Shit," Rob groaned as he rubbed the head of his cock up and down her center a few times before finally pressing it inside her eager hole. Tracey's breath hitched as Rob slowly sank inside of her, inch by inch, stretching her open around the large width of his cock.

"Oh my—Fuck," she cursed before Rob's lips were pressed over hers again, his tongue darting into her mouth as he pulled her even closer.

Rob didn't waste any time before starting up a steady pace, his hips slamming into her behind with every thrust. Tracey kept her arms wrapped tightly around his neck to keep herself from flying off the desk from the force of his thrusts. The desk creaked and screeched under their weight with every movement, and Tracey's picture frames and pen holders fell to the floor when Rob pushed her to lie on her back instead, but neither of them paid it any mind, too caught up in how good it felt to finally be with each other in this capacity.

"So big," Tracey practically purred when the two of them pulled away from their kiss, letting out a short giggle which turned into a moan the moment Rob's hand trailed up her stomach to cup her breast. "Fuck, you're—so big. Stretching me out so m-much!"

Rob let out a grunt, his hips stuttering for just a moment as Tracey clenched around him. "Tight," he gritted out. "You're tight—and wet. Can feel you dripping all over my cock. What's got you so excited, hm? What, do you like being fucked over your desk like this? I bet you do. I bet you fucking love it."

"Fuck," Tracey whined, throwing her head back as she began rolling her hips in time to meet Rob's thrusts. "Mm—Yeah, I love it! I love it, I love you fucking me o-on my desk!" She hiccuped, gasping as Rob wrapped a hand around her neck.

His grip wasn't tight enough to restrict her breathing, but it was firm enough to make all the tension practically evaporate from her body as she easily submitted to him.

Rob groaned, letting out a quiet stream of curses as he looked down at where their bodies connected and watched his cock disappear and reappear inside of her pretty cunt over and over again. His balls banged against her ass with every thrust, the sound of skin slapping against skin filling the room as he slammed into her repeatedly, and the sound was only covered by Tracey's loud moans, which Rob muffled with his mouth as he leaned down to kiss her again.

Her lips were addictive, and he couldn't resist the urge to slot his lips between hers, claiming her mouth with his own every chance he got.

Tracey tried her best to kiss him back, but she could hardly do more than hold her mouth open for him to explore as he continued pounding into her quickly, the head of his cock hitting just the right spot inside her to make her eyes roll back, her body beginning to quiver as she struggled to take a full breath. She let out a screech, her whole body jolting when Rob pulled away and licked his fingers before rubbing her clit, and she squeezed her legs tightly around his waist, her back arching as her orgasm rapidly approached.

She was so close. Right there. Just about to reach her climax when everything came to a stop. Rob suddenly stopped moving, his eyes widening as he quickly pressed a hand over Tracey's mouth. Tracey didn't understand why at first, but then she heard it.

A knock, and a muffled voice on the other side of the door calling out, "Tracey? Are you busy? Can I come in? I just have a quick question about some of the paperwork you sent me this morning..."

Tracey wasn't sure whether to laugh or cry. Just like that, her orgasm had been ruined and ripped away from her just before she managed to have it.

"Whoever that is, they're fired!" she whisper-yelled.

The annoyed look on her face was priceless, and Rob would have laughed if not for the fact that the door was unlocked and the two of them were still... connected.

"Answer them!" Rob whispered back, and Tracey huffed before clearing her throat and trying to make herself sound normal.

"I'm super busy right now! Just come back by tomorrow morning, and I'll talk to you about it then!"

"All right...Are you okay? I heard some noise—"

"I'm rearranging my office!" she shouted, her eyes widening as she looked at Rob and shrugged her shoulders.

"Okay...Have a good day then," the employee called. Silence spread throughout the room as Tracey and Rob stared at each other, chests heaving from all the exertion and from the anxiety of almost being caught.

It was at least two minutes later before either of them bothered to move a muscle, and Tracey was the first one to snap out of it, slapping Rob's chest until he got the message and moved away from her.

When she stood up, Rob began tucking his cock back into his pants, assuming that she was no longer interested in having sex in the middle of her office where anyone could catch them. But instead, Tracey ran over to her door, opened it to poke her head outside and make sure there was no one around, then closed and locked it before running back to her desk and bending over it.

"Come on," she grumbled unceremoniously. "Hurry up, I want to cum now!"

"Wow, so sexy," Rob teased.

His breath caught in his throat a moment later when she reached back to spread her cheeks apart, looking back at him as she showed off her glistening pussy. Rob growled as he stepped toward her, giving his cock a couple of strokes before lining it up with her entrance again.

Tracey held her breath and put a hand over her mouth to keep herself quiet this time, and Rob chuckled as he slid back inside of her easily.

"It's useless, you know. You'll be screaming again in just a minute."

"Oh, be quiet. Don't get too cocky because I'll have you know—" Tracey's words were cut off by the sound of her own moaning. Rob pressed a hand against her lower back to keep her down as he began fucking her quickly, pulling her hips back as he pushed his own forward, and he kicked her legs farther apart with his foot to give himself better access too.

The wind was knocked out of Tracey with the force of Rob's thrusts, and the sharp edge of the desk was digging into her stomach as he held her down with a tight grip and refused to let her squirm away for even a second, but the uncomfortable feeling was hardly noticeable as Tracey focused on the feeling of Rob's cock ramming into her G-spot over and over again.

"What was that?" Rob called breathlessly, smirking as he leaned over Tracey, resting most of his weight on her back. Tracey squeezed her eyes shut, her mouth falling open as Rob's cock was pushed even deeper inside of her with the sudden change of position. "Don't get too cocky because you'll have me know…What?"

Tracey couldn't have answered him even if she'd wanted to. She was too busy drooling and mumbling incoherently as she tried to form some sort of sentence without being able to think of any words. Her mind was completely blank as her body moved on its own accord. Her legs trembled as she stood on her tippy toes, her cunt spasming around Rob's cock as her skin burned, sweat dripping down it and mixing with his.

"Rob," she moaned in between slurred words that Rob couldn't quite make out. "Cumming, cumming—Fuck, oh my God!" she stammered before slapping a hand over her mouth again.

Rob cursed under his breath, running a hand down her back and massaging her sides as he fucked her through it. The way her body slumped, exhausted after the way her climax had been punched out of her only turned Rob on even more. She was completely pliant beneath him, loud moans turning into soft whimpers as he continued rocking into her.

"Off, off," she murmured tiredly after a few minutes, pushing at his stomach. Rob quickly slid out of her, backing away until she had enough room to stand up. She turned around to face him and dropped to her knees, immediately wrapping a hand around the base of his cock and giving him a few tugs before sticking out her tongue.

"Ah—fuck," Rob groaned, clutching the edge of the desk to keep himself steady as she pumped him quickly, staring up at him with deep brown eyes and an open mouth, ready to catch all his seed.

Rob let out another low groan before cumming with a shudder that wracked through his whole body. His cock twitched, bobbing for a moment before his cum came shooting out, and Tracey moaned as she caught every bit of it that she could with her tongue.

Rob held on to her head, watching as some of his cum dripped off her tongue and onto her chest before she closed her mouth to swallow quickly. The rest of his cum landed over her lips, and when he was finished, her tongue darted out to lick up the mess.

The moment she stood up again, Rob pulled her in for another kiss, his tongue licking into her mouth and sliding over hers. He groaned as he tasted himself in their kiss, his softening cock twitching weakly as he thought about returning the favor and eating her out.

When he pushed a hand under her thigh, trying to lift her up onto the desk again, she quickly stopped him, pulling away with a tired giggle.

"We'd better not," she murmured before pausing for a moment. "I mean, not here! One close call is already one too many for me."

"Right...You're right," Rob muttered even as he wrapped his arms around her waist, sliding his hands down her back and groping her behind.

She rested her forehead against his chest, biting her lip as his wandering fingers dipped between her cheeks, gently rubbing over her cunt before moving away again.

"So—so your place?" she squeaked.

He let out a deep chuckle that Tracey tried to pretend didn't make her want to fuck him all over again before raising a brow at her. "You want to come back to my place?"

"Well, you've been begging me to for months now," she shot back. "I guess I might as well now that I finally can...And are you really sure about that? Are you sure it's a good idea to quit your job just to—"

"We've already been over this." He shrugged. "I don't care about this job nearly as much as I care about you. I'm sure I'll be able to find something else-where. You can write me a letter of recommendation. After the way I fucked you, I'm sure you'd like to be able to sing my praises anyway."

Tracey rolled her eyes, pushing him away from her before turning to try and find her shirt among the mess on the floor. She sighed as she noticed just how much of a mess they'd managed to make. She'd forgotten all about the coffee mug that'd been sitting on her desk, and now there would likely be a stain on her floor for the rest of her time here in the office. The email that she'd been drafting before he came was now just a mess of random keyboard smashes. And the room quite obviously smelled of sex.

"I shouldn't write a damn thing for you," she grumbled under her breath. "We're gonna have to stay late just to clean this up! The one day I was supposed to be going home early..."

"You weren't complaining when I had you bent over the—Okay, I'm sorry," Rob quickly held his hands up when Tracey shot him a cold look. "I could make it up to you if you want." He wiggled his brows.

Tracey smirked. "And how are you going to do that?"

Sorry, Daddy
By Lisa Wilton-James

"Perfect, perfect, perfect," Katie murmured to herself as she ran her fingers through her red hair and fixed the tiniest smear of red lipstick on the corner of her lips. "Everything has to be perfect. Okay...Okay." She closed her eyes and let out a deep breath, shaking her head as she realized that she was being ridiculous.

She had a habit of talking to herself when she was nervous, along with running around like a madwoman and always needing to fumble with something in order to keep herself busy.

"This is fine," she muttered as she smoothed down her miniskirt and readjusted the bra-like top that she'd changed into after deciding that the previous ten shirts weren't good enough. "At least I look hot. It'll be fine."

She did look perfect.

She'd spent an almost embarrassing amount of time in the bathroom doing her skincare and pampering herself almost to the extent to which she did before going to a photoshoot or walking a runway. She'd done her makeup to perfection, with heavy liner and a dramatic eyeshadow, and with drawn-on freckles to take the place of the natural ones that her foundation had covered. She'd styled her hair just the way her man liked it–with pretty beach waves that looked effortless and flowed down her back beautifully. She'd put together a slutty outfit that she knew her boyfriend would like too. A simple, black bralette and a matching mini skirt with gold waist chains and high heels to match. William loved when she wore mini skirts and high heels together.

This was going to be fine.

"Oh my God!" she whisper-yelled, suddenly panicking when she heard William's car pulling into the garage. His least favorite car, to be exact. The one that he hardly ever drove because, really, he'd gifted it to Katie once she'd officially become his girlfriend since he never used it anyway, but Katie had begged to drive his car today instead, simply because she'd never driven it before and had always thought that it was cool.

And now...she was majorly regretting it. She wished that he'd just told her no again like he usually did. She wished she'd never opened her big mouth— *Oh, what are you so worried about? I'll take perfect care of it! It'll come back in better condition than it left in!*—Fuck. He was going to be so pissed off when she told him that she'd wrecked his precious sports car!

"Maybe it's not too late to flee," Katie murmured to herself as she eyed the front door. "I can just–"

She could hear William's keys rattling as he unlocked the door, and she had barely a second to react before it was pushed open and William was walking in, letting out a sigh. He looked tired from a long day, and once he'd hung his coat up and locked eyes with Katie, he immediately narrowed them.

"Katie, why do you look even hotter than usual?" he questioned suspiciously. "And does it have anything to do with the fact that my car isn't in the garage?"

"You're so silly." Katie let out an unnatural-sounding laugh as she scurried over to him, standing on her tippy toes to give him a kiss. "You look so handsome! How was work today? Let me grab your slippers for you!"

She slipped out of his eyesight and hustled her way over to the shoe cabinet, grabbing his slippers before practically sprinting back over to him to help him get them on.

"Work was tiring. I have a roster full of incompetent employees, which makes my job much more difficult. Why are you being weird?"

"I'm not being weird." Katie let out another robotic laugh before grabbing his hand and practically dragging him through the living room and into the kitchen. "I'm sorry you didn't have a great day, but you're in luck! I cooked your favorite meal for you, Daddy!" she practically purred, sending him a flirtatious wink before pushing him to sit down in his chair.

"Daddy?" He raised his brow. He was now even more suspicious than he had been just a second before. It wasn't like he wasn't used to Katie calling him Daddy; it was just that she usually reserved the word for the bedroom, or for when she was in the mood to get him in the mood, or for when she was teasing him about the fact that he was so much older than her, or for when she was in major trouble and wanted to butter him up before telling him whatever bad news she had to tell him. He had a feeling that it was the latter tonight. "Katie–"

"Shh, no talking." She grinned as she took a seat on his lap. Somehow, she'd managed to produce a cigar from what seemed like thin air. She clipped it, pressed it between his lips, and lit it before he could even react, then leaned toward the table to grab a shot glass and pour him a drink. "Whiskey?"

William let out a defeated sigh. Katie was nothing if not determined, and William had already had a stressful day as it was. Maybe it wouldn't be so bad to allow himself to be pampered for a little while before dealing with...whatever it was that he was going to have to deal with.

He took a puff of his cigar and nodded his head. "Yes, please."

Katie grinned, happily pouring him a shot of whiskey–and then three more once he'd finished the first. She played with the hair at the nape of his neck before allowing her fingers to travel into his thick head of hair, massaging the scalp. She pressed gentle kisses all over his face, then his neck, then his lips. She massaged his shoulders and squirmed around on his lap, pretending that she didn't realize that it was exciting him. And when she finally pulled her hands away from him, it was only to cut into his steak before it could start to get cold.

"Rare, just like you like it!" She smiled as she fed him a piece. "And I put six kinds of cheese into the mac and cheese, and I put shrimp, crab meat, and lobster meat on your loaded potato, just like you love it–Oh, and you're never going to guess what I made for dessert!"

William hummed lazily as he chewed the next bite of his steak. "What is it?"

"Red velvet cake with–"

"No." He let out a quiet chuckle. "I meant what is it? What did you do? You might as well tell me now and get it over with."

"I worked hard to cook this meal," Katie pouted, 'accidentally' grinding against William's obvious erection. "You could at least enjoy it first before asking so many questions."

William went back to chewing, deciding to humor Katie even as his curiosity piqued. He allowed himself to be handfed throughout dinner and dessert until his stomach was so full that he felt as if he might pop. The food was amazing, as much as he hated to admit it, and his eyes were beginning to droop by the time he'd finished.

Katie smiled. "Oh, you look so tired! Here, why

don't I just go run you a nice bath, and then I can give you a massage with all your favorite massage oils, and then you can go to bed feeling all relaxed and wake up tomorrow feeling well-rested and–"

"What did you do?" William repeated his previous question, tugging Katie to sit down again once she tried to stand up. He held her in place with an arm wrapped around her waist, eyes glaring into hers as he tried to read her. "Obviously, it's something to do with my car," he sighed. "Sweetheart, just be honest. If you scratched it, it's fine. It's been due for a paint job anyway."

Katie hummed thoughtfully as her eyebrows shot up in surprise. Maybe her attempt at buttering him up had worked better than she'd thought. Any other time, he would have thought of a scratch on his precious car as a life-or-death situation. Clearly, the rare steak and red velvet cake had managed to tame him a bit.

Unfortunately, it probably hadn't been enough to keep him calm while she told him about what had actually happened.

"Well, Daddy...It was a bit more than just a small scratch." She sent him a tearful look, her best set of puppy dog eyes and pouty lips.

"How...much more than just a small scratch?" His brow twitched.

"Well...Okay, so it's a really funny story, but I was at the mall earlier today, and I was just about to pull out of my parking spot when this absolute maniac came flying past, and I was terrified that they were going to hit me, so I quickly pressed the gas to go forward again and–and I kind of...Rammed into the pole that I'd been parked in front of...And now the entire front of your car is, ugh...Well, you can hardly even tell that it's a car anymore, I'm just going to be honest." She giggled nervously.

William's expression was unreadable. Katie couldn't tell whether he was pissed off, seconds away from bursting into tears, or if he'd even heard what she'd said at all. For the most part, his face was blank.

She squirmed around, this time without the intention of getting him hard. She was just uncomfortable as a heavy silence spread throughout the room and he continued staring her down with a billion different emotions swirling around in his eyes.

That car was like his baby. He'd had it for years now, and it'd been one of the first lavish gifts that he'd ever purchased for himself after becoming the

CEO of a major company. Plus, it had always been his dream car.

"I'm so sorry!" Katie cried, real tears beginning to slide down her cheeks. "Really, I am! I didn't mean to–I didn't know that I was going to–I never would have asked to drive it if I'd known that I was going to do something so stupid and–What can I do to earn your forgiveness, Daddy? I'll do anything! I'm so, so sorry, and I promise, I'll do anything to make this up to you! I know it won't be the same, but I can buy you a new one? I-I can crash my own car too? So, like–you know, like an eye for an eye type of thing? I can–"

"Ah," William hissed as she bounced in his lap, her ass brushing over his still-prominent erection yet again.

"Sorry, sorry, I'll move," she sniffled, and William's mouth formed an O shape as he thought of something.

"I know how you can make it up to me," he murmured after a while. "Well, it'll be a start, at least."

"Okay!" She nodded quickly. "Whatever you want! I'll do anything!"

He smirked. "Yeah, you will."

* * *

Don't get him wrong, he was still pissed off and majorly devastated about what had happened to his car, but this almost made it all worth it.

He'd been begging Katie for car sex for ages now, and she'd always said no because she didn't want to ruin her precious seats. But as she had said earlier, this was an eye for an eye.

"Slow down," he groaned, his voice strained as he threw his head back against the seat. "I want to enjoy it for as long as I can."

Katie narrowed her eyes at him. She wanted to argue that he'd already been enjoying himself for quite a long time. She'd given him a lengthy blowjob earlier when they'd first come out to the car, and it had resulted in him cumming all over her face, chest, and expensive leather seats. Now she was riding him in the passenger seat and had been for the last forty-five minutes. She'd already had two orgasms, and now she was exhausted, but William knew just as well as she did that she wasn't going to stop until she'd managed to make him cum too. Which is why he'd been holding out for so long.

Nevertheless, she slowed down her movements and pushed herself all the way down on his cock, rolling her hips back and forth slowly enough for her body's trembling to be noticeable. William eyed her with a lazy smile, watching as she shuddered and jolted while she continued grinding against him.

She always looked so beautiful on top, with her perky breasts bouncing together with every one of her movements, her toned stomach flexing as she tensed up, and her face stuck in a pleasured expression as she experimented, trying to figure out what felt best for both her and him. By now, she'd learned just how to ride him in order to make him cum quickly, but he'd purposely been preventing her from doing that. He enjoyed messing with her instead.

Pushing his hips up to thrust into her randomly resulted in her letting out a yelp and leaning forward to grip his shoulders as she tried to catch her breath. Reaching down to pinch her clit between his thumb and forefinger when she was least expecting it caused her to go still, her whole body locking up as her eyes rolled back. He watched closely for any sign that she was about to have her orgasm and then grabbed her hips to hold her still, effectively ruining it before it could even have a chance of fully forming.

And every time he did, he had the pleasure of hearing her cry out for him, a desperate, whimpered, "Daddy!" that went straight to his cock.

"You're so sensitive now, aren't you?" he cooed as he pushed his hand between the two of them, rubbing at her wet cunt and chuckling when she flinched and let out a whiny moan. "You're never going to be able to make me cum like this, pathetic little thing." He sent her a sympathetic look before patting her sides. "All right, up. Get in the backseat for me."

Sure, the backseat was covered in his cum, but she didn't hesitate to climb off his lap and lie down right in the center of the mess. She lay on her stomach, ass slowly wiggling in the air as she eyed him.

"Come on, Daddy," she grumbled impatiently. "Want you to fuck me now!"

He would usually tease her for being so blunt, but she looked so beautiful sprawled out on the backseat for him with her miniskirt bunched up around her waist and her high heels pressed against the window that he didn't even bother.

He pushed himself out of his seat and climbed to the back, straddling her legs and stroking his cock as he eyed her glistening, pink pussy. "Fuck," he groaned as he pushed his way inside of her again, watching as her hole stretched around his cock, taking him in easily.

Katie moaned as William leaned down, pressing

his front to her back, caging her body between his own and the sticky car seat. William reached around, hooking two of his fingers inside her mouth and pressing down on her tongue as he began moving, fucking into her with rapid thrusts, groaning in her ear as she drooled around his fingers.

"Daddy!" Katie moaned, clutching at his arm. "Shit–I'm so close, I'm so close!" she said, already shivering beneath him. Her senses were over-whelmed with the humidity that had filled the air in the car, the smell of sex, the sound of the seats squeaking as he pressed her farther into them, his deep voice filling her ears, and the sticky wetness that seemed to be everywhere. The cum still drying on her face and now on her stomach, the drool pooling around his fingers as they remained in her mouth, her own wetness between her legs making things infinitely more slippery...

Katie felt filthy and used, and she couldn't for the life of her understand why she hadn't agreed to do this much sooner, but she'd have to figure that out later because for right now, she was more interested in fucking herself back on William's cock and chasing after her impending orgasm.

"So fucking tight," William grunted, smacking her ass just to hear her squeak. "But you won't be when I'm finished with you. I'm going to fuck you until your hole is loose and abused and not tight enough to keep my big dick inside. You've got a long way to go before I forgive you for wrecking my car, sweetheart."

That didn't sound like such a bad thing to Katie. She could get used to him fucking her like this even more often.

"Wish I could cum inside you," he whispered in her ear. "You deserve to be nothing more than my sweet little cum dump." But he pulled out of her anyway, suddenly backing away from her, which caused her to whine. He was no longer on top of her, and she could already feel her orgasm dissipating as his cock slid out of her, no longer pressed up against her G-spot.

She looked back at him, wearing a sharp glare as she watched him stroke himself quickly with one hand while kneading her ass with the other. It didn't take long before he spilled all over her ass cheeks, his cum splattering over the soft flesh and rolling down between her legs soon after.

While he was panting and groaning and cursing as his body twitched and trembled, Katie was lying as still as a board, pent-up frustration making her feel as if she was overheating. The only stimulation she got was a stray drop of cum that landed on her clit, causing her hole to clench for a moment, but aside from that...she had nothing.

And she wasn't even surprised when William wore a satisfied smirk after he'd finished cumming, making no attempt to touch her again as he unlocked the car door.

"Should we head in and have a shower?" he asked.

"I hate you!" she cried. "Are we even now?"

Afterword

Hey friends! It's Rayna again.

I really hope you enjoyed this new collection. If you did, I'd really appreciate a review. It only takes a minute, and it really helps people find my work. Leaving a review is a giant help!

And don't forget to check out my other anthologies. Just search "Rayna Russell" on Amazon or Audible.

And lastly, I welcome all your feedback. Drop me an email at RaynaRussellErotica@gmail.com

And if you want to submit a story, I'd love to read it! 3000 words is the sweet spot.

Thanks again for taking this ride with me. I hope you enjoyed the hell out of it!

XOXO,

Rayna

Introduction, Volume 2

Hello again, my friends!

I had such a plethora of smut to pick from for 2023, that I had to do a Volume 2! If you're new - don't worry - you can jump into the series at any time. That's the great thing about short stories, you can enjoy them in any order.

If we haven't had the pleasure of meeting before, my name is Rayna. I am a writer and editor with a deep love for erotic fiction. I've been gathering the best short stories I could find for this series, and I'm sure you'll enjoy every one of them.

This book has quite a range of stories: from sweet and gentle lovemaking to hardcore fucking. Something for everyone. My advice: even if a story doesn't seem like your thing... give it a chance! You may discover something you didn't know turns you on.

I've listened to your suggestions!

This time, I endeavored to bring you stories from a more diverse group of writers; I've included some exciting writers of color and more stories written by men. If you're listening to the audiobook, you'll also hear some fantastic new voices that will leave you breathless.

If you have any thoughts, I'd love to hear them. Drop me a message at RaynaRussellErotica@gmail.com

And if you're a writer and want to submit a story, please do! I find 3000 words is the perfect length.

So, let's get to it! Sit back, relax and enjoy!

XOXO,

Rayna

Renée's First Time
by Renée Archer

"Seriously, Henry, I think you're doing a bit too much for me!" Renée fussed, stumbling in her steps as Henry guided her along a little too quickly. He was clearly excited about whatever he had planned for her next, and Renée was struggling to keep from tripping and falling over as she followed, tugging at the blindfold that was covering her eyes until Henry gently slapped her hand away.

"Nonsense, Renée." She could tell that Henry was smiling just from how his words came out. "I could never do too much for you, my angel. And anyway, this is the last thing, I promise."

"You said that three things ago," Renée grumbled, clumsily reaching out to smack Henry's chest.

When she had woken up this morning, she'd expected it to be an ordinary day just like any other. The two of them both had the day off work, so she assumed that she and Henry were going to spend the day lounging around the house, watching movies, reading books, or catching up on all the latest celebrity gossip.

It wasn't Henry's favorite activity in the world, but nothing made Renée's eyes light up like getting to talk about the current pregnancy and infidelity rumors, and Renée was always willing to sit and watch him play video games for hours on end despite not even being remotely interested in them, so Henry figured he owed it to her.

But instead of sleeping in until noon and then waking up to have an incredibly productive day of lounging around and doing absolutely nothing, Renée had been woken up at half past nine and told to get dressed for a nice day out.

Still half-asleep and thoroughly confused, she'd gone through all the motions of getting ready, thrown on the nice dress that Henry had insisted she wear, and then by eleven o'clock, she was in the car and ready to go. To where, exactly, she wasn't quite sure. Henry had refused to tell her where they were off to until they got there, which was a constant throughout the day.

But Renée found that she didn't mind it because each of his surprises turned out to be better than the last. They started the day out by having breakfast at Renée's favorite café, and from there, they paid a visit to her favorite bookstore and bought a stack of the new books that she'd been eyeing lately. Then they went to visit a beautiful garden that Renée had never even known they lived near. It was huge and filled with all sorts of brightly colored flowers, and there was even an area for picking, so Renée got to pick a few to have a custom bouquet made.

Honestly, Renée's day had already been more than made by that point, but Henry was only just getting started. After getting Renée's bouquet, the two of them returned to the garden and had a picnic which Henry had paid someone to set up for them. Afterward, they drove a few miles away to visit a place that Renée had been trying to get to forever: a vineyard where they did a wine tasting.

It was at that point that Renée started to get a little suspicious. She'd been begging Henry to take her there for ages, and now suddenly he was finally doing it? On a random Saturday?

"Are you dying?" Renée had questioned after

they'd left. "Am I dying? Did you cheat on me and get another woman pregnant? Are we losing the house? What's happening here?"

"Why do you think something bad has to be happening in order for me to take you someplace special?" Henry had chuckled, and Renée had sent him a bemused look.

"We don't usually go anyplace special unless it's a special occasion, but today isn't a special occasion, is it?" She'd paused, thinking for a couple of moments before she gasped. "Is it your birthday? No, that's not until December...Is it my birthday? No... It's not our anniversary so—"

"It's just a regular Saturday," Henry had told her. "And I wanted to have a fun day with you. That's all."

The simple explanation had been enough to appease Renée for a short time, but not for long. After the wine tasting, they went to the movie theater to watch a new movie that Renée had been wanting to catch, and Henry offered to buy snacks for them and didn't complain even once about the 'outrageous' price of popcorn, which only had Renée even more convinced that one of them was dying.

Then they went and grabbed dinner at a fancy five-star restaurant where they had a five-course meal. Now finally, they'd made it back home, but Henry apparently still had one more surprise–Renée was hoping that it was really only one more because he'd been saying that for a while now, and yet there was always something else. Not that she was complaining.

She'd thoroughly enjoyed the day and couldn't remember the last time they'd had this amount of fun together. Sure, they were always going out on dates here and there, but never a day-long date where Henry was willing to shell out so much cash...As much fun as the day had been, Renée was starting to get a little worried. What reason could Henry possibly have for suddenly deciding to plan such a romantic day for them?

"Did you break the Chinese vase that my mom gave us at our housewarming party?" Renée questioned, gasping as she almost tripped over what she recognized as the threshold to their bedroom. It was higher than all the other rooms' thresholds.

"What Chinese vase?" Henry pretended not to know, which only made Renée feel more suspicious. "Here, stand right...Here!" He positioned her where he wanted her to be and then let go of her arm, taking a few steps away. "Take your blindfold off in three...Two..."

"The one that you said looked hideous and swore she only gave to us to spite you because she knew that you wouldn't like it and–"

"One!"

Renée ripped her blindfold off eagerly, even in the midst of her fussing. Her jaw hit the floor and her eyes widened, her breath catching in her throat as she took in the scene in front of her. The bedroom was illuminated by dozens of little candles that were set all around, and there were rose petals covering the floor, the bed, and every other possible surface, but all of that looked dull in comparison to the sight of Henry kneeling on one knee, staring up at her with wide and teary eyes as he held a ring box in his hand.

"What–"

"I had a lot of ideas for when and where I should propose to you," Henry chuckled softly. "You know how indecisive I can be sometimes. So I decided to plan a whole day full of romantic dates for us; that way I could just whip the ring out and propose when the timing felt right. But I kept chickening out because...One of the only things that I've ever been able to easily decide on in all my years of living is the fact that I want to spend the rest of my life with you. I didn't know how I'd react if you didn't feel the same way, so I kept putting it off, but... It's time now. Renée, I love you more than words can describe. Will you please make me the happiest man on earth? Will you marry me?"

"Yes!" Renée squealed before he could fully get the words out, bouncing on the heels of her feet as she nodded quickly. "Yes, yes, yes, yes, yes! Oh my God!"

Henry let out a breath of relief and laughed as he watched her bounce around excitedly for a few moments before running into his arms. He spun her around as he pressed their lips together, neither of them able to keep the smiles off their faces even as they shared the clumsy kiss.

Henry stumbled and went flying backward, landing on the bed with a surprised grunt mixed with an amused chuckle. The two of them didn't break their kiss–what was meant to be a sweet, celebratory peck had turned into something much deeper. Something much more desperate and intense.

Renée lay on top of Henry, her arms wrapped around his neck and her body pressed as close to his as humanly possible. Henry's hands were beginning to roam a little farther down her body, and he could feel his cock straining against his jeans, already impossibly hard as it pressed against Renée's center. Whether she meant to or not, she was grinding down on it and making it even harder for Henry to will his erection away.

"Renée," he whispered after finally managing to pull away from their kiss. "Maybe we should stop before things get out of hand." He let out a strained chuckle as he glanced down at his lap and then back into her face. Her pretty blue eyes had darkened, her pupils huge as she stared at him with glistening lips and reddened cheeks. His heart skipped a beat as he stared at her, wondering if she was thinking the same thing that he was…"Or…" he murmured after a few beats of silence had passed.

"Maybe we could keep going," she whispered.

The two of them had never had sex despite being together for three and a half years by this point. They were both in agreement that it was the best idea to wait until marriage, but now…Well, technically, they had. They were now engaged to be married, and that was practically the same thing, wasn't it?

"Are you sure?" Henry rubbed her back as he searched her eyes. "We've waited this long; we can wait a little while longer if you want. There's no pressure."

"I know." Renée smiled as she leaned forward to

nuzzle her face into the crook of his neck. "I just want to be with you now. I want...to be intimate with you in a way that we haven't been before. Now seems like the perfect time anyway, I mean..." She drifted off, sitting up again to take a look around.

Today had been the most romantic and special day that they'd probably ever had together, and it had ended with a proposal that Renée had been waiting on for quite some time now. Plus, the bedroom looked like something straight out of a rom-com. If there was ever going to be a time for the two of them to lose their virginity, it would be tonight.

"Okay," Henry whispered. "Well, if you want to stop at any point or you don't feel comfortable–"

"I know." Renée smiled as she slid off of his lap to stand up again. She eyed him for a moment before tugging her dress over her head and tossing it to the side. She was stuck somewhere between feeling confident and feeling insecure as his eyes hungrily raked over her half-naked body. Sure, they'd seen each other naked plenty of times before, but this time was different. This time, they were going to be doing more than just looking.

Renée's heart pounded in her chest as she slowly crawled back onto the bed, lying down on her back beside Henry and watching as his eyes followed her every move. "You know, it's just like you to spend the day fattening me up just before we finally have sex for the first time," she half-joked.

Henry's eyes finally drifted away from the ever-growing wet patch on her underwear, snapping up to look into her eyes instead. "Hey, none of that. You look just as beautiful as you always do. Your body is perfect!" he told her, leaning down to bite her side for emphasis. Renée shrieked and jolted away from him before giggling as he sent her a smug look.

"You get on my nerves," she snickered before biting her lip as she watched him quickly take off his shirt and yank down his pants.

"It's a husband's duty," he joked, settling himself between her legs once he was completely bare. "Are you scared?" he questioned in a soft tone as he gently tugged Renée's panties down her legs. He swallowed as he watched her wetness cling to them for a moment before the thin strands snapped.

"No." She shook her head. "I've been waiting for this for a while, and I trust you. I'm excited."

"I can see that." Henry smirked as he used two fingers to spread her folds apart. Renée blushed and rolled her eyes even as she spread her legs a little wider to give him easier access. She held her breath in anticipation, waiting almost impatiently to see what he'd do.

She tensed up as he leaned forward and gave her an exploratory lick, his wet tongue sliding up her center and flicking her sensitive clit just once before sliding back down. Just as quickly as she'd tensed up, she practically melted into the mattress as he took his time exploring the most private part of her with his mouth.

His teeth nibbled on the sensitive skin around her core, his lips pressing gentle kisses all around her mound, his tongue gliding in and out of her hole, circling her clit, and flattening against her in a way that made her shiver every time. For whatever reason, Renée felt the need to try and keep herself quiet as she rolled her hips, grinding against his face without even really meaning to. Her body seemed to have a mind of its own, and that's probably why her attempts at keeping quiet were useless. Her chest heaved as she struggled to catch her breath, and her cheeks burned as noises that she hadn't even known she was capable of making slipped out of her mouth and filled the otherwise silent room. She only got louder with every finger that Henry pressed inside of her, stretching her open and exploring her insides until he managed to find her G-spot.

By the time Henry was sure that he'd taken enough time to prep her, he was trembling almost as much as she was as he lined himself up with her entrance. He was lightheaded already, overwhelmed by the thought of getting what he'd been waiting so long for. He'd spent so long fantasizing about this moment–the moment when he'd finally get to hear the love of his life moaning for him, the moment when he'd finally get to see her beautiful body splayed out beneath his, the moment that he'd finally get to see her face as he penetrated her for the first time, the first and last man that would ever get to do it–that it hardly felt real now that it was happening. But it was. It was real, and it went from feeling like some sort of faraway blur of a dream to feeling like a crushing dose of reality that Henry was suddenly hyper-aware of all within the span of a few seconds.

The way Renée's body reacted to him–the way her back arched off the bed and her legs tightened around his waist, the heels of her feet digging into his behind as she drew him in closer even while her tight cunt struggled to welcome him fully inside–made everything feel infinitely more real. There was no way he could dream up something as good as this.

"Shit," he whispered once he'd finally managed to slide all the way inside of her. He stroked her hair, leaning down to kiss her tears away as she adjusted to his size. "You're so beautiful. You feel so good."

"You do too."

"You don't have to lie," he murmured. "If it's uncomfortable–"

"No, no, I'm being honest," she cried. "It's a little uncomfortable, yeah, but not in a bad way. It's–I just feel so full, and we're so close, and I–I love you and it's just a lot but it feels good!" She sniffled, and a large smile took over Henry's face as she clung to him, wrapping her arms around his neck and refusing to let go.

"I love you too," he told her, and it was the last thing that either of them said for a while. Henry was completely still, maybe for a little longer than he needed to be, but he wanted to savor this monumental moment in their relationship for as long as he could. But he could tell when Renée had fully adjusted to having him inside of her, and he could tell when she was starting to get impatient as she squirmed around underneath him.

He squeezed his eyes shut, his cock throbbing and balls drawing up as she clenched and unclenched around him, and soon enough, it became impossible for him to stay still. His body moved on its own accord, hips bucking sporadically until he finally gave in and began thrusting into her at a set pace.

Renée's face was frozen into a beautiful expression, her shiny eyes wide as they stared into Henry's with what seemed to be amazement, and her mouth hanging open as soft moans and whimpers slipped out. Henry was more than gentle, fucking into her slowly and with shallow thrusts. Renée couldn't understand how his barely-there movements could possibly be translating into so much pleasure. Maybe it was because she was sensitive and had never done this before, or maybe it was because Henry was naturally talented in bed. Regardless, her toes were curled, her body twitching periodically as jolts of electricity seemed to course through her veins, and she was quickly becoming a mess of hiccupped moans and satisfied tears as Henry continued to grind against her.

Henry was in a similar state, panting and groaning under his breath as he rocked into her, eventually leaning down to rest his face in the crook of her neck. He could feel her wetness making a mess between them, the sheets becoming more and more soaked as the minutes ticked by, and their sweat-slicked bodies were glued together, practically molded into one as they lost track of which limbs belonged to whom.

Henry mouthed at Renée's neck, leaving wet kisses all over the sensitive skin as her nails scratched the smooth skin of his back, leaving marks that stung and only added to his pleasure. Renée let out a constant stream of whimpers, each of them more desperate-sounding than the last, and it came as a shock to them both when her body tensed up and spasmed underneath him. She gushed around the length of Henry's cock, tightening around him until his orgasm was pulled out of him too.

Renée's mix of moans and pleasured sobs mixed with Henry's low groans and curses, both of them holding on to each other for dear life, Renée's teeth biting down into Henry's shoulder and Henry's hands gripping her hips hard enough to leave bruises later.

The room seemed to be spinning even as they both kept their eyes closed and attempted to catch their breath. It would take a while for them to come down from their highs, but neither of them was in any rush. This whole day had been nothing short of perfection, and their first round of sex had been no different. If they could live in this moment forever, they would.

Renée murmured something that Henry couldn't quite understand once she finally found her voice, and he lifted his head, pressing a kiss to her cheeks and then her lips before raising his brows at her. "Huh?"

"I said I could get used to this," Renée repeated with a tired smile and star-filled eyes.

Henry chuckled. "I think I could too."

Her Recruits
by Chantal Marshall-Sisk

Carolyn had a bad habit of being nosy, which she was trying very hard to kick, but it was proving to be difficult as she found her interest being piqued by a couple of younger guys that had been coming into the bar lately.

The bar that she had been working at for the last couple of years happened to be near an army base—maybe fifteen minutes away from it at most, and definitely the closest one to it, which meant that they always got an influx of soldiers coming through, especially late at night and on the weekends.

Carolyn was always friendly enough with them, given the fact that good customer service was just a part of her job, but just like with all the other bar attendees, she wasn't particularly interested in them.

She was just here to make drinks, get her paycheck for making said drinks, and then leave. Nothing more and nothing less, on most occasions.

But recently…there had been two new faces that she'd come to look forward to seeing. Like clockwork, every Saturday night around the same time every time, they showed up.

Two handsome army friends who cracked jokes with one another over a couple of beers and some hot wings as they sat at the bar and took some time to unwind after a tiring week at the base. Their names, Carolyn had learned, were Sam and Marcus.

They both looked like movie stars with their defined muscles, chiseled faces, and charming smiles that could convince any woman within the vicinity to drop her panties in a second if they wanted her to. Their voices were deep and commanding, faces stern until the moment they decided to loosen up and start enjoying their short time off.

Carolyn had been eyeing them since they'd first started coming to visit the bar a couple of months ago, but up until a few weeks ago, she hadn't said much more to them than she really needed to. Asking for their orders and telling them to enjoy was about as much of a conversation as she'd had with them—until she'd gotten bold one night and decided to join in on one of their jokes, much to their surprise.

She'd worried that they'd be annoyed with her for inserting herself into their conversation when she was only supposed to be handing them refills for their drinks, but they'd welcomed her easily, even seemingly wanting to keep up the conversation even after Carolyn had thought it best to get out of their hair.

Ever since then, she'd looked forward to their visits to the bar even more. She spoke with them more and more each time they came, until it seemed that they'd become acquaintances, and they looked forward to seeing her just as much as she looked forward to seeing them.

Or maybe not just as much. Carolyn wasn't quite sure yet.

The guys were younger than her—maybe by a good ten or fifteen years; she wasn't sure—but she found them attractive despite her usual preferences, and she was starting to get the feeling that they felt the same way about her. She'd managed to catch them both stealing glances at her chest or her behind on several occasions, and they'd both formed a habit of staring at her lips as she spoke rather than into her eyes.

These were all subtle habits, and quite frankly, they didn't prove anything. Men would stare at practically any woman out of pure habit, even if they weren't totally attracted to her, at least that's what Carolyn thought.

But she could swear that she'd caught them whispering about her on a few occasions too. Murmuring to each other, words that Carolyn had never been able to make out because they always brought their conversation to a sudden halt when she was near.

And Marcus, the younger of the two and also the shyer, behaved like a schoolboy with a crush around her sometimes. His wide eyes and rosy cheeks were almost enough to convince her that at least he had a thing for her.

But she'd come to learn that Marcus would stare at almost any woman that way if they got close enough. She got the feeling that he hadn't had much experience with women so far.

Carolyn had been debating with herself for weeks now, trying to figure out whether they were interested in her or if she was just being delusional and seeing what she wanted to see.

But she didn't have the time to keep wondering because as she'd learned just five or so minutes ago upon 'accidentally' eavesdropping on them while fixing drinks that nobody had ordered just a few steps away from them, the two men were going to be shipped out soon, which would mean no more bar visits from them for the foreseeable future. And that meant that if Carolyn was ever going to act, she needed to act fast.

Well, that was fine. She had never been shy about asking for what she wanted before, and she didn't see the need to start now. What was the worst that could happen, anyway? They might say they weren't interested in her, and she would have to deal with the embarrassment of seeing their faces again once a week after their rejection, but just until they shipped out. That's not so bad.

Her shift would be over within the next hour anyway, so with newfound determination, Carolyn cleared her throat and walked back over to Marcus and Sam with squared shoulders and her most seductive face on. Her confidence was boosted when the two men once again halted their conversation, looking like kids that had just been caught doing something wrong as they stared at her with wide eyes.

"Sorry to interrupt—"

"You're not interrupting. We weren't talking about anything!" Marcus was obviously lying. Sam side-eyed him and let out a small breath, probably disappointed by his sheepish-looking friend's inability to lie worth a damn.

"Right. I just wanted to say that I overheard you guys talking about being shipped out earlier."

"Ah." Sam nodded. "Yeah, it's looking like we'll be leaving within the next couple of weeks. It's a shame. We'll miss coming to the bar every Saturday, and seeing our favorite bartender." He winked.

"I'll miss it too, but that's what I wanted to talk to you guys about." Carolyn smirked. "I thought it'd be nice if I could give the two of you a little...going-away present. If you're interested."

She leaned forward, resting her elbows on the bar and sending them each an innocent look, blue eyes sparkling as they stared into the men's—once they'd managed to pry their eyes away from her breasts again, that is.

"A going-away present?" Marcus's eyes darted between Carolyn, Sam, Carolyn's breasts, and Sam again as he tried to figure out whether he was reading the situation right or not. "A going-away present?" he repeated, and Carolyn couldn't help but laugh at the eagerness in his voice.

"Yes. I won't beat around the bush. I'm attracted to both of you, and I'd love the chance to show you just how much I appreciate what you guys are doing for our country before you go." She grinned. "So...I'll be off soon if you're interested, and you can meet me in the parking lot right out back. Or you can go on with the rest of your night if you're not."

She decided to leave it at that, turning away from them quickly as her heart pounded in her chest. She ignored them for the rest of her shift, serving the other customers dutifully and forcing herself not to think about what decision they made as they stood up a while later and headed out.

But all her nerves dissipated when she made it out to the parking lot after clocking out and saw the two of them standing right where she'd hoped they'd be.

The ride back to her place was a blur.

It was a short drive, and it consisted of her giving the usual spiel that she always gave to the guys she took home. *You're clean, right? You're still going to use a condom—no ifs, ands, or buts about it, but I'm just making sure. You're more than welcome to cum in my mouth but that's the only hole you better even think about spilling your seed in. I'm all for the rough stuff, but no hair-pulling, please. I have a very sensitive scalp. Spanking is perfectly fine, though, and very much encouraged.*

She talked for most of the car ride, a way for her to get rid of some of her nerves. She was pleasantly anxious as she begrudgingly followed the speed limit. It had been a while since she'd last been fucked, and now she had not one but two men to have her fun with. If she hadn't spent the whole car ride chattering, she would have combusted from the excitement.

By the time they made it to her place, Marcus and Sam were both painfully hard and impatient as they waited for her to unlock the door.

She didn't bother with any formalities as they padded inside, removing her shoes and jacket quickly after tossing her keys to the side. "Bedroom's this way. Strip, strip," she commanded lightheartedly as she walked toward her bedroom.

She was only left in her bra and panties by the time they made it inside, and Sam and Marcus were down to their underwear too.

"How do you want it?" Sam tilted his head. "Can one of us use your mouth?" he questioned as he watched her take off the remainder of her garments.

"If you want." Carolyn giggled. "But if one of you is an ass guy, then I definitely don't mind—"

"I want her ass!" Marcus volunteered quickly, his red cheeks noticeable even in the dimly lit room.

"Perfect." Sam grinned as he pushed his underwear down his legs and stroked his impressive length. Carolyn eyed it for a few moments, licking her lips before turning to look at Marcus, who slowly took his own underwear off after a moment's hesitation.

Carolyn's breath hitched, and her eyebrows shot up as she noticed how big he was. They were both more than impressive in size, but she hadn't been expecting the baby-faced boy to have the biggest cock between the two of them.

"Well, well," she practically purred. "Aren't you just full of surprises!"

Marcus's chest puffed out with pride, and Sam chuckled, slapping the boy on the back of the neck before walking toward Carolyn. "I think that's enough chit-chat. I've been waiting to have you for a long while now. A man can only be so patient."

"You've been waiting for a while?" Carolyn repeated with a grin, satisfied to know that she hadn't been delusional and that they did, in fact, like her.

"Of course I have—we both have. You're hot." He smirked as he looked her up and down. "You've been teasing us since the moment we started coming to the bar."

"Teasing you?" She put on the most innocent expression that she could muster up and shook her head. "I have not!"

"The low-cut tops and constant eye-fucking say otherwise," he growled. "Where are your condoms?"

Carolyn wordlessly pointed to the top drawer of her nightstand before looking at Marcus. "You don't have to worry about being gentle with me. I already fucked myself open with one of my biggest dildos last night," she stated almost proudly. "So do your worst."

Marcus groaned as the mental image flashed through his mind and immediately stumbled over toward the bed. He practically snatched the condom out of Sam's hand when he handed it to him, ripping the packet open as quickly as he could and nearly hurting himself as he rolled the condom over his cock.

Sam was a lot more cool and collected externally, but internally, he was just as eager and impatient as his friend was. The two of them had been fantasizing about fucking the attractive older woman since they'd first seen her, and now it was finally happening. Needless to say, he was beyond excited right about now.

He slid onto the bed, lying on his back, and Carolyn climbed on top of him immediately after, straddling him. Her breasts dangled over his face as she reached back to grab his length and lined it up so that the tip was right beneath her hole.

"Ready?" she asked, and he opened his mouth to respond, but she was already sinking down before he could. His words died on his tongue as he stifled a groan and clutched at her sides to keep her from moving. He couldn't remember the last time he'd been inside of a woman, the tight, wet heat almost too much for him to handle as he threw his head back and moaned.

His own cheeks flushed when Carolyn laughed at him, squirming around just to tease him. "What are you doing all that for? We've barely even started."

"Don't tease," he gritted out. "It's just been a while, that's all."

"Hm." She huffed out another laugh before turning to look at Marcus. He'd already lubed himself up, and now he was just waiting for the signal. When Carolyn smiled at him and gestured for him to come over, he did so immediately. She reached back to grab one of her ass cheeks, spreading it to show off her puckered hole. "Go ahead."

"Fuck, you're so sexy," Marcus muttered under his breath as he climbed onto the bed. She arched her back, pushing her ass up a little and making it even easier for him to penetrate her, and he watched with wide eyes as the tip of his cock caught on her rim, pushing its way inside slowly, inch by inch until his entire cock was buried deep inside of her ass.

Carolyn's eyes fluttered shut for a couple of moments as she huffed out a strained moan. Having two cocks buried inside of her at once, pressing against her inner walls and throbbing as they rested inside of her holes was nearly maddening. Her heart pounded in her chest, and her body moved on its own accord, rocking back against Marcus and then pressing down against Sam. She was so stretched out that she felt like an elastic band that was dangerously close to snapping, and tears stung her eyes as she sucked in a deep breath and steadied herself again.

"Shit," she let out a quiet laugh. "This is—a lot."

"Is it too much?" Sam asked quickly. "We can—"

"No, no, no. Go!" she ordered suddenly, and Sam opened his mouth to argue, but Marcus wasted no time before pulling back just to thrust into her again. He was by no means gentle as he slammed in and out of her, skipping past the slow and steady pace that Sam settled for and going straight for the rapid speed that he knew would bring them both closer quicker.

Carolyn choked on a sob as she fucked herself back against Marcus, pleasantly surprised when he wrapped a hand around her throat and forced her to throw her head back.

It was as if the two men had totally switched roles the moment they'd gotten their dicks inside of her. Marcus didn't hesitate for a moment before taking what he wanted from her, and he moved with all the confidence of a man that had been with a million women prior to her, even if it seemed as if he hadn't had much experience with women before. Meanwhile, Sam, usually so confident and seemingly sure of himself, was flustered and unsure as he stared up at her as if waiting for her direction.

If she'd had the time to feel perplexed, she would have, but she was a little too preoccupied for that now.

"Go," she repeated, the word croaked out as she struggled to speak around her moans. "F-Fuck me. Want it—Hard. Harder." She was practically pleading with him at this point, and how was he supposed to say no to that?

He snapped into action, growling as he lifted her slightly before dropping her back down, pushing his hips up to meet hers. It only took a few moments for him to sync himself up with Marcus, until the two of them were expertly pushing and pulling her between them, taking turns plowing into her holes as Carolyn tried her best to hang on and keep herself from getting too loud.

She had a feeling her neighbors would be complaining tomorrow because she was practically screaming, and no amount of lip biting and holding her breath was going to be able to stop her. She'd never felt this amount of pleasure before in her life, and this wasn't even the first time that she'd been shared between two men! Maybe it was just that Sam and Marcus knew exactly what she needed. She hadn't had to tell them anything, and yet they'd both managed to discover the areas inside of her that drove her crazy within a couple of minutes.

"I'm so close, I'm so—it's too much," she moaned, and it occurred to her then that this would be the first time in years that someone aside from herself would have managed to make her cum within just a matter of minutes. Something about that made her feel pathetically desperate and even more turned on. At this rate, she'd probably have several orgasms tonight, and by the end of it, she'd be a pile of goop and nothing more.

"Take it," Sam growled. "You can take it, I know you can."

The words weren't making it any easier for her to

hold herself together, and neither was Marcus's palm crashing down against her right ass cheek.

"Don't cum yet. Wait," he ordered, for no reason other than that he could. He wanted to see if she would listen to him, and satisfaction settled itself deep in his gut as he realized that she would.

"I-I can't," she whimpered, even as she clenched down hard, squeezing her eyes shut and trying to calm her breathing. She was trying, and that was all he needed to see in order to feel his own pleasure threatening to spill out of him at any second. He would have felt a lot more embarrassed about how quickly his orgasm had manifested itself if not for the fact that Carolyn was clearly already on the edge herself.

"Gonna pull out now," he murmured, unsure whether he was talking to Sam or Carolyn or maybe trying to convince himself. He would have loved to stay buried inside of her as he came, but she'd probably kill him if he did, and he wouldn't be able to blame her. Instead, he pulled out and made quick work of ripping his condom off and standing up to stroke himself, turning her head to face him. She opened her mouth immediately and didn't complain when he pushed himself inside, guiding her head until she began bobbing it back and forth herself.

Carolyn's movements were sloppy and uncoordinated, unlike usual, because now Sam was free to fuck into her at his own pace. He planted his feet into the bed, wrapping his arms around her waist before drilling into her quickly, and Carolyn was immediately tensing up, her eyes rolling back even as she continued sucking Marcus off.

"Go ahead," Marcus told her. "Cum all over his cock. I know you want to."

She did. Sam had to support her weight as her body shivered and convulsed, her wetness dripping all over him and onto the sheets as she came with a muffled scream.

Marcus and Sam came at nearly the exact same time just a few moments afterward. Carolyn had accidentally bitten down on Marcus's length—just a nibble. Just enough to have electricity shooting down his spine and his balls drawing up before he could even think about it. And with her repeatedly squeezing Sam's cock as if trying to milk him, Sam's orgasm was pulled out of him too. He just barely managed to pull out of her before he came. He would have loved to paint her perfect breasts with his seed, but he couldn't get the condom off in time.

He wasn't too worried about it, though. He had a feeling that they weren't quite finished for the night.

Beth Day Ever
by Stuart Goldman

Cliff drank from the bottle and glanced over at his girlfriend. She slouched against the middle of the couch, feet propped on the table, twirling a lock of hair around her index finger. Their eyes collided, and she sat up straighter and gave him a slow, sultry smile.

"What are you thinking?"

Cliff grinned. "I'm thinking about how hot you look sitting there."

Beth leaned forward, offering him ample view of her boobs in her skintight top. "How about now?"

"Hotter," Cliff replied.

He leaned over the chair and tossed the bottle onto the table. Then he pointed a finger in Beth's direction, beckoning her forward. She stood up and placed her long, tan legs onto the floor. The clock ticked in the background while she stood a few feet away. Spinning around halfway through, she bent down, giving him a generous view of her firm ass.

With a quick look over her shoulders, she wriggled.

Cliff jumped to his feet. "Don't be such a tease."

"Then it's no fun," Beth tittered breathlessly. She climbed on top of him, her back pressed against his chest. "Isn't it a lot better when you drag it out?"

Cliff made a low choking sound and rubbed his hands up and down her arms. She shuddered as he moved his hands down her front, stopping at her tight, hot crotch. Beth gasped and rubbed herself against him. With a sigh, she threw her head back and grabbed a fistful of his hair.

She smelled like peach soap and beer.

He wanted to lose himself so far inside of her, she couldn't tell where she began and he ended.

But not yet.

Before that, he wanted her so wet that her juices coated his fingers. He wanted Beth panting and slick with sweat as she begged for him. As soon as that happened, he had every intention of giving it to her, for hours on end. All of the blood rushed to his groin, and he immediately hardened at the thought of her, picturing with her legs over her head, with her ass in the air and down on her knees in front of him. The image of her running her tongue over the thick length of him nearly sent him over the edge.

Holy fuck.

"Wait." Beth pushed his hand away and scrambled to her feet. Her face was flushed, and her breathing was uneven. She placed both hands on her hips. "There's something I've been wanting to try."

"I'm listening."

"It's this fantasy I've had since I was eighteen," Beth said. She let her hands fall to her sides and moved closer to him. "And you're the only one who can help me."

"Whatever you want, baby."

Beth had a small smile on her lips. "I want you to fuck me all day."

Cliff guffawed. "Not a problem, baby. Why don't you come on over here, and we can get started?"

Beth shook her head, wisps of blond hair framing her face. "I mean literally all day. I want to be fucked every hour for an entire day."

"Holy shit. Are you serious?"

Beth waggled an eyebrow at him. "No, I'm being serious. One whole day."

"Why every hour?"

Beth pouted. "I don't know. It's just a fantasy I have."

Cliff stood up and laughed. "Sweetheart, you know how much I like to fuck you. I'd like nothing more than to do that for a while. Okay, I'm not sure how that's going to work. Even with Viagra, I could go for four, maybe five hours but not more than that."

Beth's smile grew wider, like a vixen's. "We can get creative."

"Go on."

Beth tilted her head back to look up at him. "You can use the vibrator. Any kind of toys you want. Your tongue, your fingers."

Cliff drew her to him and brought her hands up to his mouth. He sucked on each individual knuckle, his hot breath dancing across her skin. When he came to the inside of her wrist, he looked up at her and saw her parted mouth, and the hunger written all over her face.

"Is that going to be enough?"

Beth's blue eyes were wide and unfocused. "Huh?"

"For your fantasy." Cliff smirked. "Sounds like it's going to take a little more than that."

"Sounds like you want to include other things."

"Other people," Cliff corrected, giving her a heated look. "But you have to be okay with that."

Given that she was eight years younger than him and had a voracious appetite, Cliff had always known he was going to have to get creative. Even with his stamina and experience, he knew the day would come when Beth wanted more. She was, after all, insatiable at times; it was one of the things he loved most about her.

She always wanted more.

And he thrilled at the idea of giving her that.

An entire day of fulfilling her wildest sexual fantasy sounded like a dream come true, and he knew just how to make it happen. Thankfully, it was the weekend, and since it was almost midnight, Cliff had a feeling Beth had timed it exactly. Here was a woman who knew exactly what she wanted, and who made no apologies for it, and it made Cliff love her even more.

His cock twitched in anticipation.

Beth smiled. "Whatever you want. As long as you get to be number twenty-four."

"Twenty-four? As in the last person you fuck?"

Beth pushed herself up to the tips of her toes and hungrily attacked his mouth. "I wouldn't want it any other way. So what do you say?"

It took a lot of effort for Cliff took a step back. "I say take off your clothes and lie down on the kitchen counter. I'm going to go make a few phone calls."

Cliff turned around and hurried into the bedroom, where he peeled off his socks, took off his shirt, and rummaged through the drawers. When he found the handcuffs and the vibrator, using only the light of the moon, he was pleased with himself. Impatiently he took his phone out of the pockets of his shorts.

His palms were sweating as he typed up the messages.

Beth had dimmed all the lights and set up a few candles around the living room, giving it a soft, ethereal glow. Her legs dangled off the kitchen counter, her hair a wild mess around her. Jazz music played in the background. Cliff wandered over to her, pulled out the high chair, and set the toys down. He smirked as he kicked her legs apart.

Anticipation coursed through him as he lowered himself, so he was at eye level with her pussy.

He glanced up at her, and her arms were on either side of her, her head thrown back. Cliff made a low guttural noise in the back of his throat and pressed his mouth to her center. He wrapped her legs underneath his armpits, and stuck his tongue out, licking a path up to her sweet spot.

"Fuck," Beth breathed, her voice shaky. "That's good."

"We're just getting started, remember?"

Beth moved closer to the edge of the counter and huffed. "I can't wait."

"Every hour," Cliff reminded her, with a wicked grin. "I've got a full day lined up for you."

Over the next two hours, Cliff alternated between using his tongue and the vibrator, watching her face carefully. Beth had her eyes half closed, milking every minute for what it was worth. At the end of the two hours, she was covered in sweat and chanting his name underneath her breath. Thrilled, he swept her into his arms and carried her over to the couch. While she caught her breath, he placed the pill in his mouth and downed it with a large mouthful of water.

Beth had the pack of condoms in her hand when he returned.

In one quick move, he was balls deep inside of her, stretched to the hilt. She raked her fingers over his back and linked her fingers over his waist. Together, the two of them moved, the couch dipping and creaking underneath them. Cliff brought his hands up to rest on either side of the couch and dug his nails into the plush fabric.

Underneath him, she made muttered, low, and unintelligible sounds.

He threw her legs up over his shoulders and thrust, so they were chest to chest. Cliff felt the hammering of her heart against his and grinned. His own heart was loud in his ears as he pumped in and out of her. Beth came undone, shaking violently as she tried to catch her breath. A few hours later, Cliff rolled off of her and stared up at the ceiling, his limp cock covered in her juices.

Twenty minutes later, his muscles quivered as he walked into the kitchen and filled up two glasses of water.

Cliff gave her one and downed all of his quickly, anticipation making him impatient and clumsy.

When the doorbell rang, he picked his boxers up off the floor and hurried over. A short while later, their friend Lucas was stark naked and kneeling down on the carpeted floor in front of Beth. She threw her arms out on either side of her and bucked. Cliff filled another glass of water and watched her, the blood roaring in his ears.

Lucas stood up, the top of his bald head glistening as he helped Beth sit up. As soon as she did, he sat down and held his hand out. Red-faced and covered in sweat, she had never looked more beautiful or more erotic as she climbed on top of Lucas and lowered himself onto him.

Beth threw her head back and moaned, riding their friend cowboy-style.

Lucas dug his nails into her waist and rammed into her with wild and reckless abandon. He grunted and buried his face in her neck, and she made low, panting noises. Beth's head fell forward, and she looked directly at Cliff, sending desire straight to his cock. Forcefully, he set the glass down on the counter and strode over to the couch.

As Lucas pumped in and out of her, Cliff stood at the back of the couch and kissed her, thoroughly, tasting himself on her tongue. When the need for air became too great, he pressed his mouth to her neck, leaving hot, open-mouthed kisses everywhere he went. Suddenly, Beth was coming again, shaking and spasming as she did. She gripped Lucas's shoulders and bucked wildly. He jerked and shuddered against her. Once the two of them caught their breath, Beth climbed off of him and helped him to his feet. Without looking back, Lucas picked the trail of clothes up off the floor and ducked into the guest bathroom.

He gave them a smile when he came back out.

A few hours later, another one of their friends left the same way, leaving Beth with a stunned and dazed expression on her face. Cliff gave her a few minutes to catch her breath while he looked over the toys. Beth got up and rummaged through the fridge. She bit into an apple, downed a cup of iced coffee, and sauntered back to the couch. Cliff approached her, the vibrator held up to his face. She squirmed in excitement and impatience.

She spread her legs open and draped her arms over the back of the couch. "You're so fucking hot, Cliff."

Cliff knelt down in front of her and placed the vibrator on the couch. "Me? You're the one who's been at it for the past fifteen hours."

Beth's lips lifted into a smile. "Only nine more to go until you're inside of me again."

"I can't wait," Cliff whispered before reaching for the vibrator. Hours later, after a thirty-minute power nap for both of them, Cliff was harder than he'd ever been. He carried Beth into the bedroom, laid her down on the bed, and retrieved the hand-cuffs from the floor. She stared at him through lowered lashes as he spread her arms out on either side of her and cuffed them.

"Do you have any idea how sexy you were today?" Cliff climbed onto the bed and began to kiss a path up from her feet along the inside of her thighs. "I wanted to be the one fucking you every hour."

"I was imagining you the whole time."

Cliff stopped inches away from her center and covered her mouth with his. "Good because I've been waiting for my turn again all day, and I can't wait to be inside of you."

Beth lifted her hips up off the mattress. "Why aren't you?"

Cliff rubbed himself against her. "Because I want to make you as hard as you've made me."

With that, he leaned over the side and picked up a feather. His eyes stayed on her face as he ran the smooth rip over her skin, leaving goosebumps in his wake. Beth tugged against her restraints, her chest rising and falling unevenly. When she began to whimper, he settled in between her legs and kissed her. He bit down on her lower lip, and when her lips parted, allowing him access, he pushed himself into her, not stopping until he filled every part of her.

Beth groaned into his mouth.

His ears were ringing as he reached down and placed her legs around his waist. She linked her feet together, pulling him closer. He smiled into the kiss and circled his hips. Beth whimpered when he eased out and slammed back into her, causing the bed to make a low, creaking noise. Over and over, he eased in and out of her until she was covered in sweat again and choking on his name.

Beth unraveled, pulsing and writhing.

He waited until she came off her high and undid her restraints. Her arms were limp at her sides. Cliff secured them behind his neck and slowed his pace. Beth's eyes flew open when he started to move again, in practiced, even strokes. She squirmed against her restraints, and he smirked.

"Do you like it when I fuck you like this?"

"Oh, Cliff. Oh, yes."

"I want you to think of me in every fantasy," Cliff said against her skin. His tongue came out, and he licked a path up to her lobes, tasting peach-scented soap and sweat. "Because this is how it should be. You and I should fuck like this all the time."

Beth made a low choking noise and ground against him.

"Say it," Cliff urged in a hoarse voice. "Say it out loud. I want to hear you say how much you want me."

"You and I should fuck like this all the time,"

Beth repeated in a husky voice. "Oh, Cliff. Don't stop."

"I'm not planning to. I've been waiting for this all day." Cliff pumped in and out of her at a frenzied pace until she was unraveling again, writhing and panting as she did. He waited for her to catch her breath before securing her hands on top of her head. Without warning, he flipped her over and pinned her arms to her back.

Beth twisted to look at him, hunger etched onto her face. "Why did you stop?"

Cliff rubbed her ass then slapped it hard. "Admiring the view."

He eased back into her and groaned. A thin sheen of sweat broke out across his forehead. He dug his palms into the mattress on either side of him and circled his hips. Over and over, he slammed into her while she bucked backwards, his name a chant on her lips. His heart began to hammer inside of his chest, drowning everything else out, except for the sound of her moans.

Like music to his ears.

As she inched closer to bliss, he eased out and lifted her up so she was on all fours, her ass hanging in the air. He positioned himself behind her and slammed in, filling every inch of her tight pussy. Her muscles expanded and contracted against him. Cliff pumped in and out of her with wild and reckless abandon. Cliff smirked as he reached between them and found her nipples. He twisted and rolled them between his fingers, alternating between both sides until they were hard as pebbles.

Beth's head fell forward, and she let out a deep, throaty groan.

He kept one hand on her breasts, tweaking and pinching, and the other moved to her back, tracing the length of her spine. Cliff's hand moved down between them, darting in between her wet folds. When he began to stroke the bundle of nerves, Beth leaned backward and cried out. His vision went white as he undid the handcuffs and tossed them onto the bed. One arm fell to her side, and the other twisted behind her back, threading through his hair.

Cliff plunged a hand through her hair and tugged hard.

Beth did the same, sending dual waves of pain and pleasure ricocheting through him. He brought his head to a rest in the center of her back and squeezed his eyes shut. Time moved slowly as they moved against each other, hurtling closer and closer to the edge. Beth unraveled again, softer and hoarser this time as she rode out her high, her muscles quivering underneath her.

Cliff's own release followed soon after.

He squeezed every last drop into her, his body jerking as he did. As soon as he was done, he eased out of her and collapsed onto the bed next to her. A moment later, she tucked herself into his side and nuzzled his neck. Cliff threw an arm over her shoulders and released a deep, shaky breath.

"We should definitely do that again. Don't you think?"

"I love how insatiable you are," Cliff replied, pressing a quick kiss to her lips.

Happy Anniversary
by Eva Cortez

"Dinner was lovely, honey," Jared told her as he set his plate in the sink, kissing her on the cheek as he passed. "You never disappoint."

"I try not to," she laughed nervously, her palms sweating. She inconspicuously wiped them against her sides before he turned to face her again, flashing him a quick smile.

"Mm," he murmured as he approached her, pressing her against the counter with his hips and lowering his head to gently place his lips on hers. She relaxed into him as he wrapped his hands around her; this was familiar. He towered over her, so his hardening cock pressed against her stomach. "Happy anniversary."

She swallowed hard, steadying her nerves. "Happy anniversary, darling."

She loved Jared; she really did. She loved everything about him, from his puppy dog eyes to his booming laugh. He was perfect in every way. She was just nervous; since it was their ten-year anniversary, a major milestone in their lives, she had finally decided to give her husband the thing he'd been begging her for throughout their marriage.

She was going to let him fuck her in the ass.

He had been begging her for years, promising her that it would be amazing, but she remained skeptical. She knew it was going to be painful, and that was why she shied away from it, but now she was firm in her decision. Throughout their relationship, he had never asked for much, so for their anniversary, it was the least she could do.

She had ensured the kids were with their grandmother so the two of them could share an erotic evening together. She supposed it was for the best; if they were too loud during sex, there would be no one around to hear them.

He kissed her slowly, slipping in his tongue. It was sensual and familiar, and she found herself leaning into him. "Jared," she groaned, rubbing her hand against his jaw, urging him on.

Then she sucked on his tongue, pulling it further into her mouth as she wrapped her arms around his shoulders and pulled him even closer. He lifted her onto the counter, stepping in even closer, and her legs entwined around him. She could feel the hardness of him pressing against her, and her heart started to pound.

He slid a hand under the hem of her T-shirt and caressed her stomach. Her body began to quiver with anticipation.

His thumb caressed her flat stomach as his mouth made its way down the curve of her neck, nipping at her skin. His other hand tugged at the waistband of her pants, and then he pulled the T-shirt off completely and tossed it to the floor. His mouth moved to her ear, and he whispered, "I want you, Laura."

She shivered with desire, pushing her body against his. "I want you too." He unclipped her bra and removed it, but before he could take her breast into his mouth, she stopped him by placing a hand on his chest. "But I want tonight to be special, to be different."

"Okay." He tilted her head up with the tip of his finger. "What do you want, Laura? Tell me your desires, and I'll fulfill them." His eyes were hungry for her, his gaze centered on her plump lips.

She took a deep breath before speaking. "I want you to fuck me in the ass."

His eyes lit up with excitement, a grin stretching his lips. "Really? You mean that?" She nodded, and he scooped her up, tossing her over his shoulder and heading toward the bedroom. She couldn't help but laugh at his antics, both nervous and excited about what was about to happen. He tossed her onto the bed, reaching for her jeans and panties and pulling them off with ease. She watched him as he kicked off his own clothes before nimbly climbing into bed with her.

"First I'll need to warm you up," he murmured, laying himself down between her legs and parting the lips of her pussy. She already felt damp as he lowered his head, and her breath hitched in her throat when she felt his mouth. He slowly licked her clit, deliberately flicking his tongue in a circular motion along her nub. She groaned as he suckled at her, grinding herself onto him and loving the way his tongue slipped into her.

She stared down at her pussy as his mouth worked, tracing the outline of her lips with his tongue. She ached and moved her legs farther apart.

His tongue was rough against her, and it was heaven. She didn't want it to end.

And then he was flipping her over, handing her a pillow to lie on and directing her ass upwards. "This angle will be easier to start off in," he explained to her in a whisper as he moved her body. She was facing their full-length mirror, she realized. Both of them would have a full view of everything.

He reached over and rummaged in their dresser, pulling out their lube and rubbing some onto her asshole. It was cool, and she had to admit it felt nice. *Is this a preview of what's to come?* she wondered excitedly.

"I'll be gentle," he promised as he settled himself behind her, using his knee to spread her legs wider apart. Laura closed her eyes, bracing herself. She felt the head of his cock push against her asshole, and she was suddenly worried if it would fit, as he was quite large.

She gasped as he slowly slid the head of his cock into her ass, biting her lip hard to keep in her gasp of pain. Even with lube, it hurt like hell. She could feel his cock stretching her tight asshole as he pushed himself deeper into her, watching her in the mirror. She groaned in pain and clenched her hand tightly around a pillow, but she was determined to be as good as she could and not show any other signs of pain. She loved her husband, and she was doing this as a special gift. She wouldn't ruin it for him.

"Are you okay?" he whispered to her as he paused, his shaft deep in her ass. His hand stroked her hair, and she realized how tense her body was.

"Yes," she responded through gritted teeth, determined to see out her plan. The pain would go away, right? "You can keep going."

He began sliding his cock in and out of her ass, and she felt it stretching and getting bigger. Soon she was going to be able to take much more of his cock than she had previously been able to. He pulled his cock almost all the way out of her ass, then slid it back and forth along her hole and then into her asshole again. He pulled out again, and her asshole felt stretched and hot, almost burning with heat.

She groaned as he slid his cock into her again. Then he thrusted once more, and she felt him stretch her again. He put his hands on either side of her and leaned down. "I'm going to have to go slowly at this for a while, but I'm going to show you how amazing it can feel."

Then he began to actually fuck her ass at a slow and steady pace. It still hurt, but she didn't show it because he was watching her through the mirror.

He was a good husband and deserved this, so she continued to take his cock in her ass as he thrusted, his breathing heavy. He closed his eyes as he moved his hips, and she could see how good this felt for him. His dick throbbed in her ass, and she found it wasn't entirely unpleasant.

When he had fucked her ass for a while and had pushed all of his cock into her, she realized that the pain was gone, replaced by a wonderful tingling sensation, one that she even felt in her pussy. She was beginning to love the feel of his cock in her ass; it wasn't much different than when he was penetrating her pussy. When he began to fuck her faster and faster, she began to get into it more, tossing her head back and rolling her hips to match his thrusts. She began to enjoy the feel of his cock sliding back and forth inside her ass, and her asshole was getting used to his cock.

She quickly learned that she liked being fucked in the ass. She liked the feeling of her hole stretched wide and full of cock, his cock in particular. She took in more of him and begin to moan with pleasure as she continued to push back against him. She was groaning and moaning and moving with him, her breathing heavy with the intense pleasure surging through her.

"Oh God baby, fuck my ass, baby! Yeah, baby that's it, oh yeah, oh fuck yeah, fuck me," she panted, her eyes nearly rolling into the back of her head.

"You like that?" he whispered huskily.

"Oh God I'm so full, I can't take any more," she sighed. He kissed her along the back of her neck, and she tilted her head to give him better access, whimpering when he sucked on a particularly sensitive spot.

Soon he began fucking her faster and faster, and his cock was almost out of her ass when he pulled it back and then slid it back inside her again. Her asshole felt good, and she didn't know that she would ever get enough of his cock. She loved his cock in her ass. It felt so good to be filled by him.

"Oh my gosh, fuck me.... that's fucking amazing—fuck!" He dug his fingers into her as he pounded her, driving her up onto his cock with every thrust.

Her body suddenly quivered even harder, and she screamed in ecstasy. This wasn't about to end; she could feel every part of his cock pressing into her cavity, and she loved it.

As he fucked her from behind, he reached forward to grab her breast, rubbing his thumb against her nipple and tweaked it. It instantly hardened, and she purred her pleasure, the added stimulation pushing her closer to the edge.

He kept fucking her until her hips began to writhe, as though she were trying to take him deeper. Her eyes were half-closed, and she bit her lip and opened her mouth wide as she groaned, her asshole pulsing around his cock. He held on to her and made quick, shallow thrusts with his hips, which forced her ass against his cock, his cock buried as far as he could get it into her. She raised her ass higher as he kept going, taking him as deep as she could, her teeth now biting her lower lip.

She chanced a look in the mirror, noticing the way his eyes were zeroed in on her perfect, round breasts bouncing and swaying as he fucked her while his thumb and forefinger squeezed and massaged her breast. It so erotic that she could tell it took all his willpower not to cum right then and there.

He changed his rhythm abruptly, fucking her with slow, deep strokes, then faster and faster, her breathing quickening and her skin flushed. She closed her eyes and lost herself in the moment, just enjoying the pressure of his cock buried as deep as it could go as she was pushed over. Once she reached the peak of her orgasm, her whole body shuddered. Her ass clasped around him, and her eyes flew open as she cried out. As she rode her orgasm, she was lost to the sensations flooding her body.

"Oh, God, oh God!" she cried out, burying her face in the pillow. Jared was relentless, fucking her for a few more moments before pausing, his dick still deep within her as he waited for her to catch her breath.

He had to wait to catch his own breath before he let his dick slide out of her, but then he slapped her ass hard and stroked her tight little hole, and it felt so incredible that her entire body shuddered.

"Oh Jared," she managed to sigh as her breathing finally slowed. "I don't even know what to say…"

He surprised her by chuckling lightly. "Save your words, baby. I'm not done with you yet." He was back inside of her before she could speak, and whatever she had been about to say was lost in the pleasure that washed over her.

She began moaning again, pressing her ass back against him as she moved her ass back and forth with his cock. His hands were on her hips, and soon she felt his hands pushing up against her ass cheeks.

She thought that she might have another orgasm, but the thought suddenly went away as he stopped thrusting. Her thighs were shaking as he slowly slid out of her, and he slid one finger in her ass, curving it. "Oh, God. Yes! Yes!" Laura screamed.

And then Jared started spanking her ass hard. She felt a mixture of pain and pleasure, but she so desperately wanted him to do it again.

He was laughing, amused by how much she was enjoying it. "I've always wanted to do this to you!" he said. "I've always wanted to fuck your ass so badly!"

"Yes, fuck me!" she cried, wanting—no, needing it to continue. She was lusting for another orgasm. "Fuck my ass! Harder, Jared!"

Jared started spanking her hard again. He slowly circled his index finger around the outside of her ass, and she couldn't help but whimper again. "I want you to beg me for it, Laura! I want you to beg me to fuck you hard!"

Jared started slapping her ass really hard, and Laura begged him to fuck her. "Please, Jared! Please fuck my ass! Oh, please! Fuck my ass hard!"

Jared started pushing into her asshole once more. It felt so hot, so tight, and Laura was screaming into the pillow, begging him to go deeper and harder. He started fucking her harder, and Laura suddenly felt his cock being pushed all the way in. He was there!

His cock was buried deep in her asshole, and she was finally being fucked! She screamed as he pushed farther in, a strangled cry of pain and delight and satisfaction.

He fucked her slowly at first, and he kept it up for a few minutes, but then he started to fuck her harder, fucking her hard and fast. She could feel her ass grip his cock, and her asshole was stretched open, hot and wet and tight around his cock.

"Oh, God!" Laura gasped. "Fuck my ass, Jared! Fuck my ass hard!" And he did, fucking her hard, slamming into her ass, holding on to her hips and fucking her with everything in him.

He kept fucking her for several minutes, speeding up more. He pulled his cock almost all the way out, and then he slammed his cock into her ass, each thrust slamming into her hard and fast. Laura started to rock back and forth, pushing back against him, begging him to fuck her even harder. She had never wanted anything more in her life.

She was disappointed when he completely withdrew, flipping her over onto her back again. She opened her mouth to protest, cut off when he wrapped a hand firmly around her throat. "Oh!" she cried out, delighted when he slipped his dick back into her ass.

"This is a much better view," he whispered

hoarsely, his eyes glued to her bouncing tits as he thrusted.

She was close again, so deliciously close, and from the intensity of the throbbing of his cock, she knew he was too.

"Come on. Come on, baby. Let me hear you," he begged, his breathing ragged. "Come on, honey. C'mon."

He gave a particularly hard thrust that did the job, and the intense heat filled her once more. "Oh God, Jared. Yes! Oh God! Oh God! Oh!"

He kept pumping her ass, slamming his cock into her asshole again and again until finally, he could hold on no longer. His cock started twitching in her, and Laura felt the hot cum shoot inside of her. Jared's cock twitched several more times, shooting more hot cum deep inside of her. He thrust in deep one last time, squirting some more hot cum into her ass, holding on to her hips as he did.

"Oh, God," he groaned. "Oh, God, that was...I can't believe how good that felt... fucking your ass. How much I've wanted to fuck you like that for years."

"I can't believe how good it felt, too," she moaned. "Just fucking you...oh, God, I love your cock in my ass...Oh God, it was so good. You're so good. It feels so good."

Slowly, grunting as he did so, he slid himself fully out of her and collapsed onto the bed beside her.

Laura spoke as she lay on the bed next to him, her chest rising up and down with every pant. "I never knew you were that good, or I would have let you fuck me in the ass sooner."

He gave a breathy laugh. "Well, now you know."

That was incredible. Laura couldn't believe she had never considered exploring anal sex before; how could she be so closeminded? She thought over other sexual positions the two of them could do together. "That may just be my favorite sexual position yet," she murmured, rolling over to lean her head on his chest. He wrapped his arms around her, holding her close.

"Yeah?"

She nodded, smirking when his heart rate picked up. "It is. It may be the only position I want to be fucked in," she teased, though she was serious about it.

With a chuckle Jared rolled over, hovering over Laura and pressing his body against hers. His cock was stiff again, tantalizingly close to the lips of her pussy. "That's fine by me."

Dove's Porn Fantasy
by Jena Costello

Dove tried her best to memorize each of the spots where the cameras were placed as she rubbed her middle finger over her lip, fixing her lip gloss. There were a few hanging in each corner, and there were four 'passengers' holding small cameras, though they did a great job of blending in with the crowd because she couldn't see them.

She took in a deep breath as she tried to mentally prepare herself for the scene that was about to take place. She had only been working in the porn industry for four and a half months, and already, she was shooting a chaotic scene like this. Not that she didn't want to–she had jumped at the chance to shoot a video like this because this was actually one of her biggest fantasies and had been since she'd been old enough to fantasize about the way she wanted to be fucked in the first place, and when else would she get the chance to live out a fantasy like this? And legally, at that? But she always felt jittery and anxious right before the cameras came on and it was officially time to shoot.

She knew that her nerves would be short-lived because they always were. As soon as she was given the cue to start, her anxiety would evaporate into thin air as she got into character and melted into the scene. But she still hated the way she trembled and struggled to breathe before the cameras started rolling. She'd figured that the pre-shoot nerves would eventually go away the longer she worked, the more videos she filmed, and the more experience she got, but apparently not.

Fuck, I can't wait to start filming, she thought to herself, agitated as she looked around to see if they were ready to start yet. They were not. Even though the subway was already full, there were still more people crowding on to make it seem even more packed. *I'd do literally anything to be getting filled with more dick than I can handle already.*

She tried to distract herself by picking out faces. She recognized a good amount of the people that had slinked onto the faux subway. Most of them were her coworkers, some of whom she'd filmed with before, others that she'd simply seen around while she was working, and some others that she'd never met personally but had seen in videos. They were all hot, and Dove had to squeeze her thighs together as she thought about the fact that they'd all be watching her get railed at any moment now.

She checked her appearance in her handheld mirror one more time. Her makeup was perfect and would be absolutely ruined by the time she finished shooting. Her jet-black hair was pin straight, and there wasn't a single strand out of place. It contrasted beautifully with her pale skin and blue-green eyes, as did her outfit, which consisted of a simple white crop top and a white and pink plaid mini skirt.

She looked stunning, and she couldn't wait to get absolutely ruined.

It was just a few minutes later when the weight finally seemed to be lifted off her chest, relief filling the spot where her anxiety had previously been as she got the cue. All the extras were now on the set, the sound mics were all set up, and the cameras were officially on now. The scene was starting.

She stood up, wrapping her arms around the pole and pressing her chest against it as she hugged it and spread her legs ever so slightly. She stared off into the distance, pretending to be distracted even as she stared at nothing, and she could feel someone filming her from behind, getting a good shot of her uncovered cunt from below.

It had to be at least fifteen minutes that passed agonizingly slowly as they set up the scene. They filmed long shots of her body as she was pressed against the pole, getting a shot of the main male actors' faces–if she remembered correctly, their names were Logan, Trent, Jay, Drake, Jermaine, and Cole–and then filming the six of them creeping closer to her, surrounding her from all sides. By the time it was finally time for one of them to touch her, she was already dripping wet.

"Hey!" She pretended to be shocked when Trent's hand slid underneath her skirt, rubbing between her thighs. "Knock it off!" She slapped his hand away, sending him a hard look before turning to look forward again.

He moved to stand directly behind her, pressing himself up against her behind, and aside from a weak attempt at squirming away from him and turning to send him another harsh glare before looking away from him again, she didn't do anything.

Dove made herself blush as he rubbed against her behind, his erection pressed firmly against her ass as he wrapped his arm around her waist, his hand sliding up her skirt once again and cupping her cunt. She barely fought him, gasping as he spread her lips with two fingers before poking a third one up against her quivering hole.

"Stop it," she whispered weakly before biting her lip and pushing herself back against him.

"You didn't wear any panties when you knew you were going to be on a crowded subway," he chuckled in her ear. "Don't even pretend that you don't want this."

She didn't respond, aside from letting out an abrupt moan as he plunged his finger inside of her, his other hand fumbling with the buttons on his pants.

"Stop it," she tried again, attempting to turn around until he pressed her firmly against the pole again. "S-Someone might see!"

"You think they've never seen a slut getting her holes used on the subway before?" he questioned, removing his finger from her cunt in order to grab her hip and hold her still as he gave his cock a couple of strokes before pressing it between her cheeks.

Dove looked around with a panicked expression on her face, silently pleading with the first man that she managed to make eye contact with for help–Jay–

but of course, he simply smirked as he eyed her and then tapped on his friend–Drake's–shoulder to get his attention before pointing at her.

The two of them watched as Trent rutted against her, getting his cock nice and wet with her slick as he rubbed it between her lips. Dove clung to the pole and bit her lip in an attempt to muffle her moans, hanging her head in shame as she failed to keep herself quiet. She was drawing more attention to herself. Soon enough, the men that had been standing beside her–Jermaine and Logan–took notice of what was happening and decided to join in on the fun.

Dove was almost distracted from the feeling of Trent finally forcing himself inside her as Jermaine suddenly pushed her shirt up until her bare breasts were exposed and Logan stepped closer, pressing his bulge against her side and crowding her space even more.

Dove's jaw went slack as Trent sunk inside of her, inch by inch, stretching her open with his massive length while Jermaine fondled her breasts and Logan groped her cunt. Jermaine chuckled as she attempted to flinch away from him while simultaneously leaning into him as she tried to escape Logan's roaming hands as well. No matter which way she twisted and turned, there was nowhere for her to escape to and no way to avoid the men's traveling hands, so after a couple of moments, she let out a sob and went still.

Jermaine continued playing with her tits, squeezing them harshly, digging his fingernails into the soft flesh, bouncing them together as they were separated only by the pole that she was still pressed into, and pinching her nipples just to see her jolt and hear her shriek. Logan had already managed to whip out his cock and had grabbed one of her hands, forcing her to wrap it around his length and stroke him as he rutted into her closed fist.

Trent didn't give her a second to adjust to his size before beginning to pound her, his harsh thrusts forcing loud cries and moans past her lips. He grabbed a fistful of her hair with one hand, yanking her head back and forcing her to arch her back, and he kept a tight grip on her hip with the other, forcing her to fuck herself back on his cock and meet his brutal thrusts.

Meanwhile, Jay and Drake were stroking themselves slowly as they watched the free entertainment, and a few of the women around them had begun touching themselves as well while they watched. More and more people were beginning to take notice of what was going on, most of them openly staring as they began touching themselves or each other. Dove was unaware of it all, too preoccupied with trying to tame the fiery hot pleasure that was building up inside of her at a rapid pace. She couldn't cum too quickly–they didn't want her coming until she was at least on the second or third cock, and while that usually wouldn't be an issue because she'd learned to control her orgasms, for the most part, today, she wasn't so sure if she'd be able to last.

She couldn't believe that this was finally happening to her after years of daydreaming about it. Honestly, she'd been a little iffy when she'd first been contemplating doing porn for a living, but this alone could make it all worth it.

It felt as if she was having an out-of-body experience. She was so focused on the feeling of Trent ramming his cock against her inner walls that she barely noticed anything else. She heard herself moaning loudly, chanting the words *Fuck me, fuck me, fuck me* over and over again and responding to the filthy things that the men around her were saying to her with a few dirty words of her own, but she hardly realized what she was saying.

She felt something wet on her face and it took her an embarrassingly long time to figure out that it was her tears and drool. She felt something wet between her legs too, and she gasped, letting out a high-pitched moan as she realized that Trent had gone completely still. She could feel his cock twitching inside her, could feel his cum leaking out of her once he pulled out.

She wanted to complain once his length was no longer buried inside her, but lucky for her, she didn't have to. She was immediately pushed to bend over until she was face to face with Jay's dick, and he pushed his thumb inside of her mouth, pressing down on her tongue until she opened it. As soon as her lips parted, he pushed his cock inside, groaning as her wet tongue flattened against the underside of it. She gagged as he pulled her head closer, his balls slapping against her chin as the head of his cock slipped down her throat. He pulled all the way out of her mouth, giving her a few moments to cough and splutter and spit before he pushed it right back inside, beginning to face-fuck her at a brutal pace as she kecked around his length.

Jermaine was behind her, giving her ass cheeks a couple of harsh swats and chuckling with—was it Cole?—as the two took turns pushing their fingers in and out of her pretty cunt. She could make out the sound of a few voices, all saying degrading things about her and throwing loose insults her way, but she was too far gone to really pay attention to what they were saying. All she knew was that she liked it. She liked being watched and she liked being talked about as if she wasn't even there–as if she wasn't even a human, but instead, a plaything–and she liked how uncomfortable this position was for her but how enjoyable it was for the men around her, who had a great view and easy access to both of her holes.

She felt someone spitting on her holes–or maybe it was two or three people taking turns–and her body tensed up as she felt fingers prying at her asshole soon after. She'd stretched herself out last night because she knew she'd be doing anal today, but she was still incredibly tight since she didn't do anal a whole lot.

The two, then three fingers that pressed their way inside of her ass stung a little, but it was nothing that she couldn't handle, and certainly nothing that she didn't like. The pain only added to her satisfaction, but she forgot all about it a few minutes later when Jay came down her throat, pulling out of her mouth with a deep groan as he watched all his seed spill right back out and onto the dirty subway floor.

His cock was replaced with another one immediately–Logan's–and Jermaine was bottoming out inside her ass at the same time. Drake began stroking himself quickly as he stood above her, aiming for her face as he jerked himself off, and at the same time, Jermaine began slowly thrusting in and out of her, giving her a few moments to get used to his size before he began to pick up the pace.

Every one of his slow yet deep thrusts sent her body flying forward, effectively causing her to choke on Logan's cock, and Logan seemed content to stay still and just enjoy the feeling of her mouth sliding back and forth on his length as she was fucked.

Time went by in a blur as Dove barely managed to cling to consciousness. She wasn't sure whether it had been ten minutes or forty-five when several loads of cum began making her into an even bigger mess. Drake came all over her face right around the same time that Logan was coming inside her mouth–and this time, she managed to swallow at least a little bit of it before the rest spilled out. Jermaine's seed was pooling inside of her ass, dripping out and sliding over her cunt once he'd pulled out of her, right around the same time that Cole had managed to get himself off, his cum splattering all over her ass cheeks and cunt and dribbling down to the floor afterward.

Somehow, Dove ended up on the nasty floor, her cheek smushed against a sticky puddle of cum as someone held her head down while someone else pushed their cock between her lips again. Her hips were dragged up until her ass was in the air, and someone had managed to slide underneath her in order to fuck her pussy while who-knows-who fucked her ass at the same time.

This was easily the most intense scene that Dove had ever filmed. She'd never had so many cocks at once before, which is likely why when she finally did cum–if she'd had the mental capacity to be impressed with herself for holding out so long, she would have been–she squirted. That had never happened before, but it was definitely happening now. As her body drew up, shaking as she held her breath and bit her lip until it bled, she felt her pussy spasming wildly around the cock that was currently drilling into it, and she heard the hooting and hollering that started up as whoever it was pulled out of her in order to see her cum shooting out of her, drenching the floor and the men surrounding her.

She blacked out and hardly knew what was going on from them on as she was fucked through yet another orgasm, and then another one, and then another one, all of them coming quicker than the last.

She didn't manage to get her head to stop spinning until at least a few hours later when filming had stopped and she'd left the set and been pampered with a nice, long bath and expensive chocolate snacks and a peaceful massage that she slept through completely.

After a meeting with the mental health and sexual health professionals that were always kept on the sets, she was sent back to what had been trans-formed into her dressing room for the day, since she was today's star. There were flowers and stuffed animals and other cute gifts waiting for her when she got back, and nice messages from a huge group of her coworkers which she noticed after turning her phone on to check it. She would have to respond to them all later, but for now, she was just ready to change into her regular clothes, head back home, and go to sleep.

She was sore all over and bone-tired, but she also felt oddly...accomplished. And excited to see how the video turned out, which was somewhat rare for her. She didn't tend to watch her own videos on most occasions, but this one she couldn't wait to see. She couldn't pass up on the opportunity to watch herself being gangbanged on a subway, after all.

She was pulled out of her thoughts by a sudden knock on the door, which she answered with a tired "Come in!" She smiled once she saw who it was:

Daniel, the producer of today's video and the one who had suggested that she should be the star of it.

"Dove, I just came by to say that you did a great job today!" He grinned as he strutted inside, taking a seat in the chair next to hers. "Listen, after reviewing some of the footage, I was wondering...Would you be willing to do something like that again in the future? I have a feeling that our audience will love this one, and if we can get you to film something like it again–"

"No need to ask, Daniel." Dove grinned. "You already know I'm in."

She's Been Waiting For You
by Charlotte P. Grace

"And how are you feeling now, Erin?" Patrick questioned, crossing one leg over the other as he rested his pen on his chin.

Erin stared at her best friend for a moment before letting out a sigh. "You do realize that you're not actually my therapist, right?" she grumbled, sitting up on the couch. Patrick pouted as he tossed his cheap clipboard to the side.

"Well, since you won't get a real one–"

"Don't be so dramatic. I don't need to talk to a therapist just because of a breakup that I could have seen coming from a mile away anyway."

"I just don't understand." Patrick shook his head, resting his hands on his cheeks as he eyed her. "I thought you guys were doing so well! You really looked happy with him, and he seemed happy with you too!"

"Yeah, but that was just from the outside looking in," Erin sighed. "Honestly, I've been noticing that the two of us had been drifting apart for months. Instead of getting all annoyed or sulky when he decided to go and spend the night out with his friends instead of coming over to my place, I started feeling relieved. Spending time with him was starting to feel more like a chore than anything, and I know he felt the same way too. We started avoiding each other—especially alone time with each other. Honestly, I don't think he was sexually attracted to me, and I definitely wasn't attracted to him in that way either. And...I hate to admit it, but I think he might have been seeing other women behind my back."

"What?!" Patrick gasped, eyes bulging as he leaned forward in his seat. "You're kidding!"

"Nope," Erin murmured flatly. "I'm serious, I think he was. But...I never said anything because I didn't really...care."

"What?!" Patrick exclaimed again, and Erin pursed her lips for a moment before shrugging her shoulders.

"I really mean it when I say we drifted apart. I

don't know how it happened–you remember how the two of us were in the beginning. We were all over each other all the time, we couldn't keep our hands off one another, we couldn't go more than an hour without seeing each other or else we'd lose our minds...But that feeling faded away not too long after we'd officially started dating, and we ended up becoming pretty much indifferent to each other. He didn't care what I had going on, I didn't care what he was out doing, and I guess the only reason the two of us even stayed together for so long was just because it was easier than having to break up. For a while, at least, but then our awkward, five-minute-long conversations started to feel unbearable, and I guess he just got tired of it and finally decided to put an end to things, which I'm kinda grateful for because I know I never would have been able to. I've never broken up with a guy before."

"Erin," Patrick huffed, standing up from his chair and coming over to plop down next to her on the couch. "Why didn't you tell me about this sooner?! I'm your best friend in the whole entire world–at least, I'd better be–and even I didn't know that this was going on. I seriously thought you two were made for each other!" he grumbled, wrapping an arm around Erin in an all-too-tight hug.

Erin giggled as he squeezed the breath out of her. "I don't know. It just didn't seem like something that I even needed to talk about, if that makes sense. I wasn't sad about it or anything, and you know the two of us never really talked about him when he wasn't around because there was always other gossip to talk about instead." She grinned.

"Mm," Patrick hummed. "You're right about that. You know, I still have to tell you about what Amanda and Tyesha ended up in jail for last Saturday. You'll never believe what happened–"

"Before we get to that..." Erin laughed, pulling away from her friend and beginning to play with her hands. Patrick narrowed his eyes at her, well aware that she was suddenly looking a lot shyer than she had been just seconds before, and Erin could feel the man's gaze burning the side of her face as her cheeks flushed.

"What is it?" he questioned curiously.

"Well, you know how you're gay...and all?"

"Ugh, yeah?" Patrick snickered. "I'm aware of it, yes. Why?"

"Well...It's just that I kind of think that I might be too–"

"What?!" Patrick jolted away from her, his hand shooting out to clutch at his chest. Erin rolled her eyes at her best friend's dramatics, but admittedly, she couldn't blame him too much for his reaction this time around. They'd known each other for years, and this was the first time that she was mentioning being anything aside from straight.

"Don't make a big deal," she warned him before continuing. "It's just that I kind of...I think that's part of the reason that I became so uninterested during my relationship. I hadn't been with many guys before him, and definitely not for a long time before they all ended up breaking things off with me for one reason or another–"

"Mm, right. Found another girl, had to move away, and found out he was gay, all in that order, right?"

"Right." Erin side-eyed him, pouting. "So anyways, Michael was my first real, long-time boyfriend, and the first one that I ever thought I loved, and the first one that I ever did anything sexual with and...I don't know, it just didn't feel right. I wasn't into it, I wasn't into him, and I started to notice that I was a lot more interested in the girls than I was the guys when we'd watch porn together–"

"You two watched porn together? I've never

done that with any of my boyfriends. I'm too jealous."

"That's beside the point." Erin waved him off. "The point is, I think I may be interested in girls, but I've never been with one, and I've never had the chance to experiment, and...I kinda really want to. But I don't know how to go about finding someone–"

"Hello?" Patrick sent her an incredulous look. "The answer is right in front of you!"

"Um..." Erin eyed Patrick, narrowing her eyes. "You're gay, not a lesbian woman. How would you possibly be able to help me out in this situation?"

"You're so dense sometimes," Patrick murmured as he slapped a hand against his forehead. "No, I mean–you definitely came to the right person for help, but you could have cut out the middleman if you'd wanted to. Don't you remember that a certain someone by the name of Paloma exists?"

"Paloma?" Erin raised her brows. "I know she's a lesbian, but that doesn't automatically mean that she's the solution to my problem. I don't even know if she's into me, so I can't just go and ask her to let me experiment with her."

"Erin, please." Patrick sent her an exasperated look. "If you went to her and asked her that, it would make her day. Her year, even. Paloma's been waiting for a moment like this since she first met you! She's so into you that it's honestly sickening."

"What?!" Erin's eyes widened almost comically. "Really?! Why didn't you tell me?!"

"I thought you knew! Everyone else sure does," Patrick muttered. "And it's not as if she's been particularly discreet about how she feels toward you. The constant touching, the plethora of dirty jokes–the way she looks at you as if you're the last piece of meat in the supermarket. Doesn't she always send you pictures of her in her underwear? Hasn't she literally told you that she would fuck you before?!"

"Well–but–" Erin spluttered, cheeks starting to burn even hotter as she thought back on all of her interactions with Paloma. "I thought she was like that with everyone! I just thought that she was a super touchy, flirty, dirty joke-telling person who enjoyed sending people pictures of herself regardless of what she was wearing. And I thought that her telling me that she'd fuck me was like a hypothetical thing, like–like, 'Oh, yeah, I'd fuck you I guess if I had to.' You know, that sort of thing!"

"You're hopeless and grossly oblivious, and I love you," Patrick sighed as he took out his phone. "I'm going to text her and tell her that you and Michael broke up. Everything will fall into place from there.

You won't have to lift a finger–believe me, she'll come running the moment she realizes that you're now a hundred percent available."

Erin hated it when her best friend was right. At least on most occasions, but she was very happy that he'd been right this time around because it meant that she didn't have to fret over trying to find someone to experiment with, and honestly, she'd always had a teensy tiny crush on Paloma that she'd previously refused to acknowledge anyway, so it was nice to know that Paloma was apparently very into her too.

Apparently very into her.

She'd responded to Patrick's text immediately, telling him that she was on her way to Erin's apartment. She'd quite literally beaten Erin back, even after stopping to pick up a bouquet of flowers for her.

Erin was a flustered mess as she struggled to unlock the front door to her apartment and welcomed Paloma inside. She remained a flustered mess for the hour and a half that the two of them had spent talking in the living room. Paloma pretended to be sorry that Erin and Michael had broken up, and

Erin explained that it was very much okay and that she was more interested in enjoying her newfound freedom as a single, potentially gay woman…

They ended up in Erin's bedroom in record time.

"I don't have that much sexual experience under my belt," Erin was rambling as she clumsily pulled her clothes off. Her head got stuck in her shirt for a few seconds longer than she would have liked, and she nearly fell face-first as she struggled her way out of her shorts, but Paloma was kind enough to pretend not to notice. "I mean with men. I have none with women. But I already said that…" Three or four times. She was just trying to prepare Paloma. She didn't want the woman to expect too much from her.

God, what was she going to do? How did lesbian sex even work? Well, she knew how it could work– she'd watched plenty of lesbian porn, but…But she wasn't as flexible as some of those women were, and scissoring seemed like an Olympic sport. One that she had not yet trained for and best not attempt. And as much as she hated to admit it, she was not yet at the point of feeling comfortable enough to put her mouth anywhere near someone else's vagina. So that was out of the question too.

"Babe, just relax." Paloma sent her an easy smile that Erin tried to mimic. "I'm not expecting you to know the ins and outs of everything when you haven't ever done this before. Just don't worry about anything and let me take care of you, okay?"

Erin swallowed thickly, trying to ignore the butterflies in her stomach and the odd throbbing between her legs.

This was off to a good start. She was already turned on, and they'd been in this room for less than three minutes. That was great.

"Okay," she agreed easily.

Paloma gestured for her to get on the bed, and Erin did, awkwardly climbing on and laying down on her back. She was completely naked and sprawled out like a starfish, which she became hyper-aware of once Paloma's gaze darkened, her eyes wandering Erin's body freely and catching on the plump mound between her legs.

Erin attempted to close her legs just a little, and Paloma's brown eyes immediately shot up to stare into her blue ones, narrowed ever-so-slightly in a warning look that made Erin stop moving immediately.

Paloma's lips twitched up into a pleased smile as her eyes trailed back down, and Erin's entire body felt as if it was on fire as she lay there and allowed herself to be looked at. It was an uncomfortable feeling, having someone staring at the most personal part of herself, but not 'bad' uncomfortable. More like... unusual. But kind of hot. Especially since Paloma seemed to like what she was seeing.

The longer she stared, the wetter Erin got.

"We'll start simple." Paloma's voice finally cut into the thick silence after a while. "With something that you're probably already familiar with. Mind if I eat you out?"

Erin felt as if she was melting. She cleared her throat, at a loss for words as she shook her head. She couldn't believe how blunt Paloma was, and she wished she could be like that too.

Erin did eventually end up finding her voice when Paloma had settled herself between her legs, pushing Erin's legs to rest over her shoulders.

"Oh—I meant to say I haven't—it's not exactly familiar." She let out a nervous giggle. "I've never been eaten out before either. But that's okay! I still want you to—"

"Michael never ate you out while you were together?" Paloma raised her brows and sighed when Erin shook her head. "Men. What the hell are they even good for?"

Erin would have laughed if Paloma hadn't pulled her closer and dived in right in at that moment.

Erin's back shot up off the bed as soon as Paloma's lips dragged along the center of her cunt, but Paloma pushed her to lay back down before dragging her tongue down her slit and flattening it against her hole.

Erin gasped, eyes widening as she watched in awe. Her chest was already heaving, back already arched as she stared down at Paloma, who was staring right back up at her.

The foreign feeling of having a warm, wet tongue pressed against her pussy would have been enough to overwhelm her as it was, but on top of that, Paloma was staring up at her with deep brown eyes, lust swirling in them as she mouthed at Erin's cunt. Her chin was already wet with Erin's slick, and Erin bit her lip as she stared at the pretty woman, her cunt throbbing with even more vigor as she took in the naughty sight. Just staring at Paloma propped up between her legs had her head starting to spin.

"Shit," she nearly whispered as Paloma gave her clit a few kitten licks before dragging her tongue between her folds in a 'Z' formation. When she made it back down to Erin's hole, she slowly pushed just the tip of her tongue inside, and it was enough to make Erin squirm. "Paloma!" she whined, only semi-embarrassed by how worked up she was getting already.

Paloma seemed pleased, letting out a quiet chuckle as she pulled her mouth away from Erin's cunt. "You're so cute, babe." She massaged Erin's hip for a moment before dragging her hand over Erin's stomach and down to her cunt. "I'm just getting started."

Erin's mouth fell open as Paloma thumbed at her clit, rubbing it gently as she spread Erin's lips with the fingers of her other hand. Erin's body flinched and seemed to melt into the bed when Paloma allowed her spit to dribble off her tongue and onto Erin's pussy, and then she leaned in, pushing her tongue inside of Erin's hole again and wriggling it around until Erin let out a choked moan.

Erin's body moved on its own accord, her hips rolling forward to grind against Paloma's face, her thighs drawing closer to Paloma's head and tightening around it as she held the woman in place.

"I—Oh my—Fuck!" Erin threw her head back, clutching the sheets in her fists as she squeezed her eyes shut and tried to remember to breathe. She could hear herself moaning, but she couldn't make herself stop no matter how hard she tried—and she couldn't remember ever being this vocal in her life.

She'd been practically silent on the few occasions that she'd had sex with Michael, but she'd assumed that it was just because she was a silent partner.

Apparently not.

Michael had never made her feel this good. Hell, she'd never even managed to make herself feel this good.

Her orgasms usually came after thirty minutes or so of her touching herself, and they were always short-lived and, for the most part, not worth the effort. It was three seconds of pleasure that dissipated almost as soon as it came and left her feeling like she'd just wasted her time for no reason, and afterward, she'd get up and carry on with her day as if nothing had even happened.

But this time, Erin's orgasm crept up on her without her even knowing. All of a sudden, she could only see stars, she was crying and borderline screaming, her body was bucking and spasming against her control, and she hardly knew what was going on until she realized how wet the bed suddenly was, and how her hole was clenching around nothing repeatedly without her even trying, and how Paloma had removed her tongue from her cunt and was instead kissing her way up Erin's body until she made it to her lips.

Erin didn't have much of a concept of time, but she couldn't understand why she still felt as if she was coming when it had to be at least a few minutes later. She was rendered speechless, and all she could do was stare up at Paloma as Paloma talked to her in a soft voice, saying words that Erin couldn't comprehend.

Then Erin's eyes were widening as she felt a finger slipping inside of her, and then another one. Then Paloma's lips were pressed against hers, their mouths glued together as they exchanged a wild kiss, and Paloma's fingers were pounding in and out of Erin quickly, and before she'd even come down from the last high, she was sent right back into orbit as Paloma coaxed another orgasm out of her.

Thirty seconds after the first? Thirty minutes? Erin wasn't quite sure.

Time seemed to fade away as they continued kissing, and Paloma continued playing with Erin's wet pussy while rubbing her own against Erin's hip.

Erin could tell when Paloma came by the way her jaw suddenly went slack and she struggled to kiss back. She suddenly went still on top of her, her fingers no longer rubbing at Erin's clit.

Erin was exhausted by that point and hardly able to keep her eyes open, but a lazy smile still settled on her face as she realized that Paloma had gotten to cum too. She felt proud. Even if she hadn't done much to assist her, at least Paloma had gotten off. Erin was determined to make that happen again soon, but for now, she was too tired.

"Are you okay?" Paloma's voice was muffled as she buried her face in Erin's strawberry blond hair. "You liked everything, right? How do you feel?"

"Like I'm on top of the fucking world"—which was ironic because she was still lying beneath Paloma, and now Paloma's entire weight was pressing her into the mattress which was making it a little difficult to breathe, but Erin was certainly not going to complain. "I loved everything that happened. I want it to happen again!"

Paloma giggled, cuddling Erin impossibly closer. "Me too."

The BBQ
By Clay Roth

Pete wiped the sweat off his face. Wrinkling his nose, he dropped his hand and reached for the beer bottle on the counter. He lifted it up to his lips and took a few sips, cursing the heat as he did.

He squinted and used the tongs to flip the meat onto its back, waving away the mist as he took another swig of beer.

Sweaty and impatient, he spun around, eyes sweeping over the backyard until they landed on his wife, standing with one hand on her shorts-clad hips, the other nursing a glass of red wine. She smiled at her friend, took a sip, then threw her head back and laughed.

Pete couldn't take his eyes off her.

Although all the other women in the room were

wearing provocative clothing, given the extremely hot weather, she was still the only one who could pull it off effortlessly. Her jean shorts showed off impossibly long, tanned legs, and her strapless top clung to her body, showing off a good amount of cleavage.

Suddenly, Pete couldn't wait for everyone else to leave.

He wanted to be balls deep inside of her, even after three years of marriage.

"How's it going?" Bill materialized by his side. "It smells good."

"Yeah, the trick is to marinate it overnight."

"No shit?"

Pete gave his friend an annoyed look. "Yeah, Penny was the one who told me that if you leave it overnight in the marinade, it sucks it right up."

Bill nodded. "Smart. Penny knows her shit."

"She does," Pete agreed with a smile. "She's a hell of a cook."

"She is."

"And she is smoking hot," Pete continued with another glance in her direction. She looked over at him and smiled, her tongue darting out to lick her ruby-red lips. Pete straightened his back and winked at her. Penny's smile turned wicked as she ran her lips over her mouth again, slower.

Holy shit.

Pete's cock twitched, and he had no idea how much longer he was going to last.

Bill's voice drew him back to the present, forcing him to fix his attention on the meat, and the two of them made small talk while waiting. Finally, he loaded the meat up onto the trays and carried them over to the table set in the middle of the backyard. Penny paused to make sure there were enough plastic plates and cutlery before coming to stand next to him. He placed a hand around her waist and pressed a kiss to her cheek.

"Have I told you how amazing you look today?"

"A few times."

Pete's hand drifted down to her ass, and he squeezed. "Well, you do. I haven't been able to stop looking at you."

Penny twisted her head to look at him, a mischievous sparkle in the depth of her eyes. "Well, you'd better stop, or we might have to do something about it."

Peter chuckled and moved so she was pressed against him. "I have half a mind to take you inside right now. Forget about the guests."

Penny leaned forward, and he caught a whiff of her floral perfume. "I don't want to be rude to our guests. They'll be gone in an hour anyway."

Pete groaned. "I don't know if I can wait that long."

Penny placed a hand on his chest and pressed her mouth to his ear. "If you do, I'll make it worth your while, I promise."

Pete drew her in for a hug and rubbed his hard length against her. "You have no idea how hard you're making me right now."

Penny laughed and rubbed herself against him. "I think I have a pretty good idea. Down, boy. We can have some fun as soon as everyone is gone, okay?"

Pete bit back another groan. "Fine, but they have one hour. After that, I'm going to start kicking people out."

Penny drew back and touched her lips to his. "I'd expect nothing else."

With that, she stepped out of his arms and turned to face their guests, chatting and laughing with everyone else. She positioned herself so her back was covering him, hiding his erection from plain sight. After a while, it got better, and she moved to sit at the table with everyone else. For a while, Pete watched, a low buzzing in his ears until he stood up straighter and went around to the head of the table. Up in the sky, the late afternoon sun was blazing, nothing but clear, blue skies for miles on end. A warm breeze drifted past, smelling of earth and sunflowers.

He exhaled, sat down, and started to wolf down his food, leaving crumbs everywhere.

Penny sat next to him, bathed in a soft halo of light and talking to a redhead next to her. Now and again, she touched his knee underneath the table, her touch scorching through the thin fabric of his boxers. He kept picturing himself draping her over the table and having his way with her whenever her hand drifted too close to his crotch. Pete saw her with her flimsy bra, legs spread open, and his mouth between her thighs.

Pete could taste her juices already.

Instead, he bit into his food and counted the minutes until people began to trickle out. An hour later, he was on his fourth bottle of beer, a faint buzzing in his ears and a warm trickle in the center of his stomach. Everyone else was gone, except for Bill, who was helping them clear up. As soon as he was done, he pulled up a chair and sat down next to Pete, who kept eyeing Penny as she bent over to pick up discarded plastic cups.

"Looking good, honey," Pete called out. "I'm really enjoying the view."

Penny wriggled her hips. "I'm glad you approve."

Pete leaned back into his chair. "Damn, isn't my wife hot?"

Bill touched his beer bottle to his lips. "Yeah, she is. You're lucky, man."

"You're goddamn right I am. Penny is so hot I know that every man wants to fuck her."

Bill sat up straighter. "That doesn't bother you?"

"Hell, no. I'd love to watch, if you know what I'm saying." Pete glanced over at Bill, who was staring at his wife, a strange gleam in his eyes. "Do you want to fuck my wife, Bill?"

Bill's eyes grew wide. "I didn't mean any disrespect, man. I don't want any problems."

Pete clapped Bill on the back. "What problems? I just told you I'm okay with it."

Bill stared at him. "Are you being serious?"

"Come over here, baby," Pete called out, his eyes never leaving Bill's face. Penny climbed on top of him, her ass settling comfortably on top of his dick.

She pressed her lips to his and kissed him deeply. The beer bottle fell to the ground with a thud as Pete growled, his hands moving to her waist. A short while later, she drew back and looked over at Bill.

"You want to have some fun, Bill?"

Bill swallowed, his Adam's apple bobbing up and down. "This isn't a trick?"

Pete grinned. "Have some fun, Bill. Don't you think he should, baby?"

Penny stood up and sauntered over to him. She sat down on top of Bill and rubbed herself against him. His hands remained at his side, his pupils dilated. As quickly as possible, Pete took the beer bottle out of his hands and set it down on the floor. Penny began to press hot, open-mouthed kisses along the side of his neck. Bill's hands moved to her behind and squeezed.

"There you go," Pete goaded with a smile. "She has an amazing body, doesn't she?"

Bill released a deep breath. "She does."

Penny framed his face in her hands and kissed Bill squarely. Then she ran her fingers through his thin, blond hair. Bill began to pant, so Penny drew back and stood up. She held a hand out to him, and he took it, letting her lead him through the glass doors and into the living room. Pete picked up the beer bottles and hurried in after them, a familiar strain beginning in his shorts.

He watched as his wife pushed down her shorts and took off her top, leaving her in lacy black underwear and a bra. "You look so fucking sexy, Pen."

Penny blew him a kiss.

She gave her hips a little extra sway as she walked over to Bill, who was fumbling with the zipper of his shorts. Emitting a high-pitched giggle, she helped him push his shorts down so they fell down to his knees. Carefully, she bent down and removed them before doing the same to his shirt, all of them falling into a heap on the floor a few feet away. Pete's heart began to pound in his ears when she knelt down and began to kiss Bill again.

With his heart hammering against his chest, Pete wandered over to the armchair facing the couch and sat down. He crossed one leg over the other and placed a hand on his crotch. Through the fabric of his shorts, he rubbed himself. Meanwhile, Penny continued to gyrate against Bill, who was making a loud moaning noise. Eventually, she took his hand, placed it on top of her underwear, and moaned.

Pete thought he was going to explode then and there.

He pressed his lips together and leaned forward.

But he wanted more.

He needed more.

Pete wasn't going to be satisfied until another man stuck his dick inside of his wife and fucked her senseless. And he grew harder at the thought of it.

In one quick move, Penny reached behind her back and undid the clasp of her bra. As soon as her breasts spilled forward, Pete's mouth went dry. He swallowed when Bill buried his head in her chest. Bill took one nipple between his teeth and tugged, hunger written across his face. Penny threw her head back and moaned when he moved on to the other one. Then he pressed and kneaded until they were both covered in sweat.

Damn.

Penny had never looked hotter to him.

Watching his wife with another man was the most erotic thing he'd ever done. Bill moved his hands up and down Penny's arms, pausing at the small of her back. She made a low, throaty sound in the back of her throat and stood up. Her back faced her husband as she bent down to slide off her underwear, pausing to kick it away. Pete gripped the armrests and dug his nails there.

Bill jumped to his feet and pushed down his

boxers, allowing his erection to spring free. "Shit, I can't believe this is actually happening."

"You better believe it," Penny said in a sultry voice. "I can tell you've been wanting to do this for a while, haven't you?"

She grabbed him and pulled him toward her. "You like fantasizing about other men's wives, don't you?"

Bill groaned. "Fuck, yeah."

"Good." Penny released him and pushed him away, so he fell back onto the couch. "Pete is watching us, Bill, so I want you to fuck me hard and fuck me good, okay?"

Bill's eyes darted over to Pete before they went back to her. "Okay."

"Good boy." Penny climbed on top of him, and he eased into her. She threw her head back, placed her hands on either side of the couch, and whimpered. Bill dug his nails into her waist and thrust forward, stretching out inside of her.

"Fuck, you're so tight, Penny."

Pete stood up to push down his shorts and his boxers. He sat back down and touched himself, unable to look away from the two of them. Penny began to bounce up and down, growing louder and louder while Bill filled every inch of her. Before long, she came, writhing and spasming on top of him. Bill kept thrusting, making loud grunting noises as he did.

Penny placed her hands on his shoulders and shook her head.

Pete kept touching himself, imagining Penny's smooth and deft fingers instead of his own.

Bill stopped, and she stood up, motioning for him to do the same. She sat back down on the couch and swung her legs over the side. As soon as she draped herself over the entire length of the couch, she twisted her head to the side and looked directly at her husband. Impatiently, Bill climbed on top of her, settled in between her legs, and eased back in.

Penny called out his name.

Pete's blood was roaring in his ears, his movements growing faster and more pronounced.

Bill threw Penny's legs up over his shoulders and circled his hips. "Fuck, yeah. This feels better than I thought."

"Yeah? Do you like how tight I am, Bill?"

"I do," Bill ground out, his face a bright tomato red. "So tight and so wet."

Penny kept her eyes on Pete's face. "Do you like how good I feel?"

Bill made a low, strangled noise in response. She

raked her fingers over his back and squeezed her eyes shut. A thin sheen of sweat broke out across her forehead. Over and over, Penny ground against him, taking, so they were both moving with animal-like abandon. Pete stood up and pushed his chair closer, the screeching noise reverberating inside of his head.

Together, they both turned to look at him and smiled.

Pete smirked, sat back down, and pulled off his shirt. Penny's eyes flew open, and her eyes went to her husband's face as she reached between her and Bill and touched herself. Bill lowered his head and took a nipple into his mouth. He sucked and tugged until Penny was panting and chanting underneath her breath. He moved to the other nipple and did the same, so Penny was twisting and writhing underneath him.

Fuck.

Pete wasn't sure how much longer he could take it.

But he didn't look away, especially when Penny came again, her body spasming and writhing violently. As soon as she caught her breath, Bill climbed off her and held his hand out. Wordlessly, she took it, and Pete saw the excited gleam in her eyes when Bill spun her around and positioned himself behind her. She placed both hands on her knees and looked over at Pete, her green eyes filled with hunger and mischief.

Bill's gaze settled on Pete's as Pete sat back in his chair and smiled. "Are you enjoying yourself, Bill?"

Bill straightened his back and eased himself into Penny. "Your wife is so hot."

"She is," Pete agreed. "Don't stop fucking her."

Penny made a noise of agreement and used one hand to push her hair out of her eyes. Without warning, Bill eased out and slammed back into her. Again and again, he moved until Penny began to grow impatient and twisted her arms behind her back to reach for him. Bill pinned her arms over her back and grunted.

Her breasts bounced up and down as he thrust in and out of her.

They moved quickly, making low whimpering noises that filled every inch of the living room. Pete grew harder and harder, blood pounding against his ears. A short while later, he leaned forward again, smiling when he saw Bill reach forward, two fingers darting in between Penny's wet folds.

Penny threw her head back and moaned.

Bill dug his fingers into her scalp and tugged. "You make me so hard, Penny. Shit. Do you even know how hot you are? What a tease you are. Always wearing those short, tight outfits...Fuck."

"Oh, God." Penny squeezed her eyes shut. "Oh, Bill. Fuck me. Come on, fuck me harder."

Bill released her arms and gripped her hips. "Do you like that your husband is watching us?"

Penny's eyes flew open, and she looked over at Pete, a wicked smile hovering on the edge of her lips. "Yes. Pete loves watching me fuck."

Bill grunted. "Does he like watching other men fuck you? Sliding their thick cock over and over into your wet pussy?"

Penny let out a long, throaty moan. "Oh, God, yes."

"Yes what?"

"Yes, he does," Penny breathed, her eyes moving over the length of Pete's member before it moved back up to his face. "Don't you, baby?"

"Keep fucking," Pete said in a strained voice. "Don't stop. Fuck, you're so sexy, Pen."

It kept building up within him, the feeling growing stronger and stronger.

Bill buried his face against Penny's back, his thrusting growing wilder and more frenzied. Penny reached behind her and rubbed a hand up and down his arm. She made a low, panting noise as they moved together, moving closer and closer to the edge. Suddenly, she grew still and placed both hands back on her thighs. She ground backwards, eliciting a growl from Bill. He dug his nails into Penny's waist and said something into her skin.

Moments later, she threw her head back and cried out, her entire body shaking as she came undone. Bill thrust a few more times before he his body began to shake too. She held still and waited for him to come undone before he eased out of her. Moments later, she sauntered over to Pete, got down on her knees, and took him into her mouth.

The entire length of him was inside of her mouth while she moved her full, sensuous lips over him. Pete's hands moved to cup the back of her neck. He kept one hand there, and the other threaded through her hair. She licked and sucked, making growling noises in the back of her throat. Pete lifted his hips up off the couch and pushed himself all the way in.

She lifted a hand between them, playing with the hair on his chest.

Suddenly, his entire body jerked and spasmed.

Penny swallowed and smiled up at him.

When he was done, she lifted herself up off her feet, knelt between them and kissed him soundly. He pulled her onto him, gripped her waist, and deepened the kiss. She made a low sighing noise and rubbed herself against him.

"Does this mean I get to watch this time?"

Penny drew back and tossed Bill a look over her shoulders. "We'll see."

Whatever You Want, Sir
By Joe Parks

"How was work?"

"Shit," Ben replied, pausing to remove the tie from around his neck. He tossed it onto the table by the door and exhaled. "I feel like I don't know what the hell I'm doing anymore."

Evie looked up at him. "What do you mean?"

"Those new guys are really busting my balls. And they're making me look really bad while doing it."

Evie wandered over to him. "I'm sure it's not that bad. You've been there for years anyway. Your boss knows how hard you work."

Ben drew her closer. "I'm not sure it matters. Not when those guys come from money."

"I'm sure you're better than they are anyway."

Ben smiled. "Yeah? What makes you say that?"

"Because I know you." Evie stared at him through hooded eyes. "Not only are you smart and ambitious, but you're also twice the man they are."

"Yeah?"

Evie's hands moved from his shoulders, tracing the length of his back. "Definitely."

Ben smiled. "You always know what to say to make me feel better."

"How about a massage?"

"Does that include a happy ending?"

"If you behave," Evie teased.

She stepped out of his arms and spun around. His eyes stayed on the sway of her ass until she came to a stop in the middle of the kitchen. While she opened and closed several cupboards, his hands moved to the zipper of his pants. He stepped out of them before kicking them away. Ben unbuttoned his shirt, his fingers moving quickly and deftly till it fell to the floor with a flutter.

He had changed out of his clothes completely when he brought one leg up to rest against the chair. Evie was humming underneath her breath and running her fingers through her dark hair. She set up several candles on the kitchen counter with a smile. When she looked up, her eyes widened in surprise.

"That was fast."

Ben shrugged. "I like a woman who knows what she wants."

Evie smiled and pushed her hair out of her eyes. "I like a man who knows what he wants."

"Why don't you come over here and show me how much?"

Evie's smile turned wicked. Without saying anything, she pushed herself off the counter and flicked off the lights in the kitchen, plunging them into a state of semi-darkness. The candles flickered and moved, casting long shadows across the walls and bathing Evie in a warm, ethereal glow.

She came to a stop in front of him, wrapping both of her arms around his torso. "God, you're sexy."

Ben brought his hands to a rest on her ass and squeezed. "So are you."

Evie pushed herself up on the tips of her toes and touched her lips to his. "I'm going to go get some of that massage oil."

"Or we could do other stuff," Ben suggested, pausing to give her behind another firm squeeze. "I know something we can do that's a lot more fun. I can give you a hint if you want."

"We'll get to that," Evie promised with a shake of

her head. She drew back and disappeared down the hallway and into the bedroom. As soon as she did, Ben walked over to the couch and placed the laptop down on the coffee counter. He smiled and draped the comforter over the back of the couch before settling on top of it.

Once he was comfortable, he heard the wooden floors creak.

Evie's floral perfume filled the air a few seconds later. "Are you ready?"

Ben looked up and over at her. "I'm always ready for you."

Evie gave him a slow, sultry smile and squeezed the bottle in her hand. Lathering her hands with oil, she crept toward him. Once she spread a thin sheen of it over his back, she stopped. Out of the corner of his eye, Ben saw a flash of movement, and when he looked over his shoulders, Evie was naked. Her tanned skin glistened underneath the candlelight.

He hardened at the sight of her, and his cock twitched.

She climbed onto the couch and brought her hips to a rest in the middle of his back. Evie began to knead and press against the muscles of his back, pausing every so often to press a kiss to the back of his neck. She left a trail of heat in her wake until she slid lower and draped herself over his back. Her nipples were pressed against his back, as firm as pebbles. Ben made a low growling noise in the back of his throat.

Her fingers moved to his shoulders, and she pressed hard.

Everywhere she touched, he felt like he was on fire.

But he wanted more.

In the distance, he heard cars honking and tires screeching against the asphalt. He lifted his head up, but she firmly pushed it back down. "Don't worry about anything else."

"All you have to do is enjoy yourself," Evie murmured into his back. She pressed her mouth to the back of his neck, her hot breath sending shivers racing up and down his spine. "Forget about the world outside, okay?"

"Okay."

Evie smiled against his neck. "Good. That's it. Do you want more pressure or less pressure?"

"More," Ben replied huskily. "I love how your fingers feel on me."

"Want me to do some exploring?"

"Please." Ben groaned when she dug her elbow into his lower back. It wasn't long before she removed the pressure and used her fingers to press down. She then moved back up to his shoulders, shifting her hips so she was leaning over him. In silence, Evie kneaded and stroked until Ben felt like he was putty in her hands.

Little by little then all at once, her movements grew slower and less pronounced until she stopped altogether. The couch creaked and dipped as she got up and came to a stop next to him. Ben tilted his head to the side, and his vision grew focused. She reached behind her and held up a pair of handcuffs, the silver glistening as it moved back and forth.

"How do you want me?"

Ben jumped to his feet. "Are you sure about this?"

"Whatever you need to relax. Tonight, you're in charge, baby, and I'm all yours. So you get to call the shots here."

"We need a safe word."

"Peaches."

Ben's pulse quickened. "Get on the couch and lean back against it."

Evie gave him a quick kiss before she did as she was told. She sat so she was looking up at him, a thin trail of sweat collecting between her breasts. "What do you want me to do now?"

"Sir," Ben told her, his heart pounding against his ears. "You have to add sir to the end of every sentence."

"What do you want me to do now, sir?"

"Touch yourself," Ben said with a lift of his chin. "But don't cum unless I tell you to."

"Yes, sir."

Ben lowered himself so he was at eye level with her. "You're going to be a good little girl, okay?"

"Whatever you want, sir," Evie said breathlessly. She brought one hand up to her face and trailed it down so it was resting between her breasts. Evie then pinched and tugged on the nipple. When she was done, she moved to the other one, making it impossible for Ben to look away. All of the blood rushed to his groin. He pressed his mouth to hers and growled.

Once Evie moved to deepen the kiss, he pinned her arms on either side of her. "Not yet."

Evie's tongue darted out to lick her lips. "Okay."

He used one hand to pick up the handcuffs on the couch and the other to stroke her face. His eyes never left her face as he lifted her hands up over her head and secured them in the handcuffs. Ben gave them a firm tug before he got up and glanced down at her. Her chest was rising and falling unevenly, and her eyes were wide with excitement.

"Where are you going, sir?"

"I'll be right back," Ben promised in a husky voice. He spun on his heels and hurried into the kitchen. There, he swung the freezer door open, cold air crystalizing in front of him before it disappeared. He reached for the ice cube tray and used his shoulders to close the door. Ben pulled out a cup and emptied some of the cubes there.

When he made it back to Evie, she was squirming and impatient.

He took one cube between his mouth, placed one hand on either side of her, and knelt down. Using his mouth, he moved the cube over her flushed skin, his stomach tightening when she gasped. Goosebumps broke out across her flesh, and she began to whimper. She linked her legs over his middle and tugged him closer.

Ben spat out the cube. "You're not supposed to do that."

"I guess I'm not such a good little girl after all, sir," Evie whispered, her eyes swimming with desire. "You need to punish me, sir."

Ben kicked her legs open and settled in between them. He brought his mouth so it was in front of her center and blew. Evie tugged on her restraints and cried out. With a smirk, he dug his nails into her waist, and his tongue darted out to lick her. She was wet and ready for him, and her juices tasted better than anything he'd ever eaten. It was a rich slightly sweet flavor he couldn't get enough of. His eyes rolled to the back of his head when her legs tightened around his waist.

The sound of her whimpers was like music to his ears.

Once she was close to the edge, Ben stopped and looked up at her. Slick with sweat and through hooded eyes, she glanced down at him. "Why did you stop, sir?"

"You're being punished." Ben threw one leg up over each of his shoulders and positioned himself at her entrance. In one quick move, he was inside of her. Evie threw her head back and moaned, the sound reverberating inside of his head. He thrust deeper into her, until her muscles began to expand and contract.

"Oh, Ben. Oh, yes."

Ben grew still and looked down at her face. "What did you call me?"

"Sir. Please don't stop."

Ben grunted and circled his hips. "Good. You've been a bad girl, haven't you?"

"Mmm, yes, sir."

"And I'm the only one who can punish you."

"Yes, sir."

"Say it," Ben urged in a strangled voice. He gripped her feet and spread her legs apart. "Say it so I can hear you."

"No one else is man enough to punish me," Evie gasped out before squeezing her eyes shut. "I need you to punish me, sir."

Ben growled and pressed kisses along the inside of her thighs. "I'm going to keep punishing you until you're begging me for more. Do you understand?"

"Yes, sir."

Suddenly, he stopped and let her legs fall back down on the couch. Evie made a low protesting sound, and her eyes flew open. Her mouth parted when he leaned between them and kissed her soundly. She sighed and moved to deepen the kiss. He swept his tongue along the bottom of her mouth before wrenching his lips away. Ben spun her around so her back was facing him. Evie settled onto the couch, bringing her bound hands to a rest against the couch.

"You're so wet, Evie," Ben murmured into her back. His hand moved between them, and he stroked her. "Do you want me to fuck you?"

"Fuck, yes."

"Fuck, yes what?"

"Fuck, yes, sir," Evie replied, her voice dropping an inch. "I want you to fuck me long and hard, sir. Till I'm begging and screaming for you."

Ben growled. "Good because that's exactly what I'm going to do."

Without warning, he eased out of her and slammed back in, earning a loud moan. Ben eased in and out of her until she was panting and calling out his name. Each time he got closer and closer to the edge, and it took every ounce of energy he had to stop. Whenever he did, Evie tugged against her constraints and made whimpering noises to protest.

He gripped her hips and slammed into her hard.

It wasn't long before his pace changed, and he began to move with wild and reckless abandon. Evie's pants grew labored until her entire body shook and spasmed against his. Ben held her still and slowed while she rode out her high. As soon as she grew lax, he began to move again, slower this time. Evie ground and bucked against him, hair whipping around her face and plastering itself to her forehead.

She came undone again, calling out his name as she did.

Ben waited until she caught her breath before he eased out of her. Immediately, he flipped her over so she was draped over the couch. He kicked her legs open and settled in between them, his mouth finding hers. For a while, he only kissed her, framing her face in his hands and stroking her soft skin.

Evie tasted like bubble gum flavored toothpaste.

And he loved every part of it.

Once he nipped on her lower lip, her mouth parted, and his tongue darted in. Soon, there began a sensual battle for dominance, with Evie struggling to get the upper hand. When she failed, she sighed and melted, every inch of her fitting against him. Finally, he wrenched his lips away and began to press hot kisses along the side of her neck. She lifted her arms up over her head and wriggled against him. He used one hand to hold hers in a vise-like grip, and the other trailed down the length of her body, stopping at the inside of her thighs.

He pinched the flesh there, and she jolted. "You're mine, Evie. Do you understand?"

"Yes, sir."

"No man is ever going to make you feel the way I do," Ben added before he inserted one finger in between her wet folds. She bucked against him, a thin sheen of sweat breaking out across her forehead. He added another finger and began to stroke her, coating his fingers in her juices.

Draped on the couch underneath him, Evie was completely at his mercy.

She lifted her hips up off the couch and bucked against him. Ben drove her closer and closer to the edge only to stop. When she blew out a breath of frustration, he bent down to kiss her. Then his movements shifted so he was targeting her sweet spot.

Evie moaned into the kiss.

She twisted her head to the side and called out his name as she fell, her entire body shaking as she did. Ben watched her carefully and pressed his bulge against the side of her legs. When Evie's vision cleared, she looked directly at him and smiled. Without warning, she spread her legs further and linked them over his behind, squeezing and ushering him into her.

In one quick thrust, he was inside of her again.

He shifted so he had one arm on either side of the couch and pushed into her. As soon as he was all the way in, he began to move again, easing in and out of her with ease. Evie brought her bound hands to a rest in between them, stretching her fingers so she was stroking his smattering of chest hair.

Ben kissed her and growled.

Without warning, he undid her handcuffs, and her hands went to his shoulders. She kneaded the muscles there, pressing and pushing as she did. Evie wound her fingers through his hair and tugged hard. Waves of pain and pleasure ricocheted through him. He buried his face in her neck and inhaled, the smell of peach-scented soap washing over him.

Evie raked her fingers over his back, leaving marks in her wake.

She stopped at his ass and squeezed hard.

His mouth parted, and he began to leave wet, hot kisses along the side of her neck. When he stopped, he parted his mouth and grazed the other side. She shivered and shuddered against him, ripples breaking out over her skin. He dug his palms into the couch and rammed into her. Evie lifted her hips up off the couch, meeting each thrust with one of her own until the couch was dipping and creaking underneath their weight.

Over the pounding of his heart, he could hear the sound of skin slapping against skin and smell their sweat as it filled the apartment. Eventually, he squeezed his eyes shut and circled his hips, his movements growing faster and more frenzied. It wasn't long before Evie came again, chanting his name as she did. His own release followed soon after, and he waited until his body stopped jerking. Once it did, he eased out of her and collapsed backwards onto the couch.

Evie crawled next to him and brought her head to a rest against his chest. He shifted and wrapped an arm around her shoulders. She pressed a kiss against his chest over the thundering of his heart and sighed.

"We should definitely do that again," Evie murmured in a low voice. "I like this side of you."

Ben's mouth lifted into a half smile. "Yeah? I like this side of you too. You were very sexy."

"So were you, but I have a request for next time."

Ben glanced down at her and smiled. "What is it?"

"I want to be the one calling the shots."

"Oh, no. Have I created a monster?"

Evie laughed and pinched his arm. "If you have, you're just going to have to deal with it. You have no one to blame but yourself."

Ben cupped the back of her neck and kissed her. "I'm sure I'll find a way to manage."

Jade
by Stefanie Jones

Jade grinned as she looked herself over in the bathroom mirror once again to make sure that she still looked perfect—which she did. Her chocolate-colored skin was as smooth as a baby's bottom and shiny from the lotion that she'd rubbed all over herself. Her curly hair was freshly washed, the usual frizz no longer present after the hours she'd spent carefully styling it to perfection.

Her makeup had come out looking great too. She'd chosen to go with a bright red lip and white eyeshadow, plus plenty of glitter and highlight. It brought out her hazel eyes and matched her white lingerie nicely.

She usually wasn't one to wear sexy lingerie, but tonight was a special occasion. She and her husband were trying to spice up their sex life a little bit, and wearing something sexy to bed rather than her usual plaid pajamas was one of the first and easiest methods that she'd thought of.

So she'd dug around in the back of her dresser drawers until she managed to find something that her husband had never seen her in before: a two-piece bra and panty set that consisted of a white lace bra that her breasts spilled out of and a matching pair of panties that barely covered her ass.

She paired it with a matching choker and a thigh garter and the knee-high socks that she knew her husband loved to see her in, and she could hardly keep the wide smile off her face as she eyed herself in the mirror. She looked sexy, and she knew it. Her husband would love it!

She took a deep breath before finally turning to walk out of the bathroom and strutting into her bedroom instead. She stood in the doorway, striking a sexy pose and laughing when her husband let out a low whistle once he saw her.

"Damn," Trent said as he sat up in bed, his eyes tracing her figure hungrily. "You look amazing, baby!"

"Thank you," Jade giggled, biting her lip as she

looked Trent over as well. "You do too." But Trent always looked incredible, in her opinion.

He was easily the handsomest man that she'd ever laid eyes on, with his piercing green eyes, tan skin, and sandy blond hair, not to mention the fact that he had the body of a Greek god. Muscles and abs for days! And his gorgeous body was on full display, only his underwear covering his lower half. Jade's mouth watered as her eyes caught on the large imprint in his tight-fitting underwear...Only the thin piece of fabric hiding what she wanted to see the most...She had half a mind to go over and rip them off with her teeth.

"Come here," Trent ordered, and Jade's stomach fluttered at the sound of his soft, raspy voice. She didn't hesitate for a second before tip-toeing over and crawling between his legs, settling herself on her knees as she waited for his next command.

It didn't come anytime soon. Trent was just content to stare at her, his eyes raking over her exposed skin slowly, goosebumps forming underneath his gaze.

Jade tried not to squirm as her skin heated up and a shiver traveled down her spine. She had always been the shy type, and they almost always had sex with the lights off, their bodies hidden underneath the covers the whole time. It was no wonder why Trent was staring daggers into her rarely visible skin, but that didn't make her feel any less embarrassed about it.

Oddly enough, the flustered feeling only seemed to make her feel even more excited. She liked having his eyes observing her. She liked the way they burned a hole in her flesh—and unapologetically at that. Trent didn't have the decency to feel embarrassed about openly eye-fucking his wife, and something about that had Jade's cunt clenching around nothing.

Maybe she was just exceptionally horny.

At this point, Trent simply blinking at her could turn her on. They hadn't had sex in over a month because life had been pretty busy for them lately, and secretly, Jade had been enjoying the wait. The longer she went without having her husband's hands on her, the more desperate she became. And sex was always best when it happened between two desperate fools.

"You're so perfect," Trent practically whispered as his hands slid up Jade's sides. Jade's breath caught in her throat as the man's gentle hold and feather-soft touch suddenly became a death grip, his hands squeezing her tightly and his fingertips digging into her flesh as his eyes traveled up to stare into her own wide ones. The corner of his lips slowly turned up into a smirk as his half-lidded eyes sparkled with cruel amusement. "I want to ruin you."

I

"You're just too easy," he snickered, shaking his head. "Doesn't take much to get you going, does it?"

Jade eyed the hard-on between his legs for a moment before quirking a brow at him. "You were rock hard before I even stepped into the room. Should you be talking?"

Trent chuckled, squeezing her sides hard enough to make her wince before pulling his hands away completely. Only for a second. Only long enough to push his underwear down his thighs and allow his cock to spring out, rock hard, veiny, glistening with precum already.

Jade's mouth watered as she stared at it, a billion different thoughts entering her head all at once. She wanted to touch it, to stroke it, to rub her thumb along the slit to collect the white pearls forming there. She wanted to lick it, to have her lips stretching around it, to have the tip of it gagging her as it pressed against the back of her throat. When Trent wrapped a large hand around the base of it,

Jade wanted to smack his hand away and grab it herself.

But she only had a few seconds to stare before Trent was grabbing her waist again, dragging her forward and pushing her legs apart in order to make her straddle him. She gasped, steadying herself with her hands resting on Trent's shoulders, and her eyes widened as Trent rested his hands on her behind and pushed her up just enough to be able to get a good grip on her panties and rip them right apart.

"Trent!" she cried, torn between fussing at him for ripping a still practically new pair of panties and moaning as he rubbed the tip of his cock between her folds a few times to get it nice and wet. Her entire face felt as if it was being burned off as she hid it in the crook of his neck. This was much different from how things usually went.

Usually, it was soft hands and delicate touches carefully removing each other's clothes, Jade lying on her back and welcoming Trent on top of her, hardly able to see him in the darkness of their bedroom as they made sweet love until the early hours of the morning.

Now Jade was the one on top, half-dressed but feeling fully exposed with Trent's cock pressing against her uncovered cunt and his hand fondling the breast that he'd reached up to pull out of her bra. She felt like a slut, getting felt up and fondled so unceremoniously, and the feeling only intensified as she realized just how much she liked it.

"How could I not be hard?" Trent murmured. "Look at you. So pretty for me, baby...Sit."

Jade's body followed the order before her mind could even register it, and the wind was knocked out of her as she slid down Trent's length until she'd taken it all inside. With no previous preparation, the slide stung, and her breath came out staggered as she panted against his neck, the sudden full feeling almost too much for her to handle.

But she always loved how overwhelmed she felt once their bodies were connected again for the first time after a long while. She always insisted that there was zero prep, no stretching, no lube, no nothing. She loved the burn and the way her body was forced to adjust to Trent. The way his cock nestled against her insides and made room for itself among her internal organs.

Sometimes, she could swear that she could feel him in her stomach—Trent thought that was a little dramatic but it certainly stroked his ego, so he wasn't going to complain.

"Oh my God," she whispered, sucking in a sharp

breath as Trent readjusted her ever so slightly. The two of them were otherwise still as Jade tried to adjust to the sudden intrusion. Trent massaged her back gently, throwing his head back to rest against the headboard as he tried to keep himself under control.

"It's been way too fucking long," he growled, and he didn't give her the chance to respond as he grabbed her head, pulling her in for a bruising kiss. Jade moaned as his teeth clanked against hers before their mouths opened against each other, tongues dipping into each other's mouths, tangling together and lips smacking together repeatedly.

She felt lightheaded as Trent controlled the kiss, pressing their mouths together firmly and refusing to allow her to come up for breath for even a moment. Jade loved when he got like this—so wrapped up in what he wanted that he disregarded what Jade wanted and forced her to take whatever he chose to give her instead. It was only a kiss, but already, Jade was letting out needy moans, tears wetting her lashes and threatening to spill down her cheeks as her body began buzzing with delight.

It was a few minutes later when the two of them began moving, Jade rocking back and forth and swirling her hips around in small circles, Trent's hands resting on her hips, controlling her movements as he ground against her. Just enough to press himself a little deeper inside of her, just enough to have her struggling to catch her breath even more than before as she moaned and whimpered into his mouth. When Jade lifted herself up just slightly before pressing herself back down against him again, Trent knew that she was ready and didn't hold himself back for a second longer.

Jade gasped, her mouth falling open, lips still connected to Trent's only by a thin string of spit as he finally pulled away from their sloppy kiss in order to focus on lifting her up with his hands beneath her thighs and slamming her back down again.

Jade's face scrunched up for a moment before falling into a relaxed expression of pleasure, her eyes half-lidded and staring into Trent's with practically nothing behind them, her mouth still hanging open and brows furrowed ever so slightly as she let out a quiet giggle mixed with a moan.

Trent took that as his signal and started up a steady pace, easily lifting her up and down on his length, bucking his hips up to meet her. All Jade could do was cling to him, doing her best to hold on tight as he pounded into her without mercy, his cock stretching her open and slamming against the bundle of nerves inside of her with every thrust.

Trent was nothing if not skilled when it came to pleasuring his wife in the bedroom. He'd come to know her body more than she did. He knew just what to do, just the right way to move in order to drive her crazy. He knew what each and every one of her facial expressions meant too.

When he grabbed her ass, spreading her cheeks apart and squeezing them until he was sure his knuckles had turned white, she winced as his fingernails scratched her flesh, and she let out a choked moan, staring at him with teary eyes that seemed to be begging him not to let go.

When he leaned forward to take her nipple into his mouth, swirling his tongue around it a couple of times before sucking on it, and his eyes traveled up to stare into hers again, she could hardly hold the eye contact because she was struggling to keep her eyes open as her body quivered and her chest heaved. It was easy to overstimulate her, and she was already more than halfway there.

With his wet tongue resting against her already sensitive nipple, his fingernails digging into her skin and causing her flesh to burn and his cock steadily splitting her open, she was more than overwhelmed.

And she couldn't resist the urge to use one of her hands to tweak her other nipple, the other still clinging to Trent's neck to keep her from flying off him.

"Close," she moaned, her voice cracking. She didn't need to tell him because he already knew. The way she tightened around him, squeezing him so tight that it was getting harder to keep up his pace. The way she bit at his shoulder when the pleasure got to be too much and absent-mindedly bucked against him, silently pleading with him to go harder. The way she murmured incoherently under her breath in between curses and moans. Trent knew that she would cum at any second.

Without any warning, he changed their position, pushing her to lie on her back and folding her practically in half, her knees resting underneath her chin as he slammed into her, balls slapping against her ass, her wetness dripping down his length every time it reappeared briefly before disappearing inside her again.

Jade's head was spinning from the sudden change, and it took a few moments for her to figure out whether she was right side up, upside down, on top of him still, or now underneath him. She could hardly find it within herself to give a damn regardless. All she knew was that there were stars dancing in front of her eyes, Trent's low voice was in her ear growling filthy words that she didn't have the mental capacity to make out, and he was crowding her space, overwhelming every one of her senses.

His voice was all that she could hear, his musky scent was all that she could smell, and every part of her body was being touched by his. His hands rubbing the backsides of her legs and hooking beneath her knees, his cock drilling into her and mixing up her insides, his mouth eventually pressed firmly against hers in yet another messy kiss.

Him leaning over to kiss her was what finally sent her over the edge. His cock being fucked even deeper inside of her had her crying out before she could think about it, her muscles locking up and her back arching as she trembled and spasmed beneath him. Trent didn't slow down but continued to pound her with rough thrusts that totally contrasted with his suddenly soft tone of voice as he talked her through it.

"There you go," he whispered. "There you fucking go. You've been waiting for that for a while, haven't you? I bet it's all you could think about, and now here you are. You got what you wanted, baby. You finally got to cum for me, huh?"

Jade was mostly unresponsive aside from the occasional attempt at a nod, but that was perfectly fine with Trent. He liked when she got like this—her bones turned into putty, drool pouring out of her mouth, her eyes blank as she blinked at him, her mind in a whole other dimension.

"Cute." He let out a fond chuckle and then a low groan when she clenched weakly around him. It was only a matter of minutes before he was spilling inside of her with a couple of grunts and muttered curses, his eyes squeezing shut as he rested his forehead against her shoulder and tried to catch his breath.

His muscles burned and ached from the intensity of his orgasm, which had ripped itself out of him with little to no warning, but that didn't stop him from lifting Jade up a few minutes later and carrying her off to the bathroom.

It seemed like such a shame to be stripping her of her pretty lingerie when he'd hardly gotten to enjoy looking at it for more than a couple of minutes, but her naked body was infinitely more beautiful, especially under the steady stream of water once he'd helped her into the shower.

He watched for a while as the water cascaded down her brown skin, water droplets seemingly teasing him as his eyes followed them down her chest, over her breasts, her stomach, and between her thighs.

He really hadn't intended on doing anything aside from helping his wife get cleaned up after their vigorous night of sex, but was it his fault if he got hard again while staring at her perfect figure?

Jade let out a tired giggle, not surprised when Trent wordlessly lifted her up and pressed her against the wall. She wrapped her legs around his waist and her arms around his neck, ignoring the way her sore muscles resisted her movements.

"Again? Already?" she questioned as Trent pressed himself up against her, slowly lining himself up with her entrance again. He knew she was teasing more than asking, but he merely sent her an unimpressed look as he slowly slid inside of her again.

A smug expression came onto his face as she moaned and melted against him, turning into a pile of mush yet again the very moment that he'd bottomed out.

He would be repeating her words right back to her not a full ten minutes later when she was squirming desperately as she was fucked against the wall, screaming about how close she was to coming again.

Dear Cara
by Phillip Andres

Dear Cara,

I wonder if you're in class right now.

I thought about calling you, but I wanted something a little more intimate. Letters have a much more personal touch, don't you think? And I wanted something you could read over and over while picturing me writing it. I want you to be able to sniff the paper when you're done, looking for a whiff of my cologne.

But don't let that distract you from your classes.

You should be in your dorm room when you read this, preferably in your room with the door closed. I know you like to leave it open while you sit around in your lacy underwear and tank top, but you know how much I hate that.

I hate imagining someone else seeing you like that, even if it's just your roommates. Since it's a co-ed dorm, I spend too much worrying about it, and I don't want to know. No one but me should be able to see that much of you, leaving little else to the imagination.

Are you turned on now?

Because I am.

I'm sitting in my office at home, in only my boxers, and I'm touching myself.

You should be too.

All I can think about is the last time you were here, and how you showed up in that ridiculous over-sized trench coat and combat boots. Do you remember my reaction when I opened the door in my stained hoodie and sweatpants? I still can't believe you spent an entire car ride in nothing but the trench coat and boots.

Just thinking about you driving naked, bathed in nothing but moonlight, turns me on.

Fuck.

Do you have any idea what you do to me? Or how crazy you make me?

I bet you do.

You and that mouth of yours drive me crazy, especially when you're down on your knees sucking on my cock. I've been thinking about that the past few weeks, and how good it felt when you spent an entire weekend riding me. Those two days were the best days of my life, and I keep replaying them in my head and seeing your tanned, glistening body on top of mine, your breasts bouncing up and down.

I can still hear your whimpers in my head and feel your fingers move over my skin, as if were marking me.

God, you're so sexy.

Are you touching yourself right now?

I hope to fucking God you are.

Because I want to touch you right now.

I want to touch you so badly I might just explode.

I've been thinking about this long and hard, and I want to make it up to you. I've been imagining you getting home from college, in your tight pink sweatpants, your emblazoned hoodie, and your hair piled on top of your head. I can see the smile on your face, and your gasp of surprise when you recognize me there, draped over your bed in nothing but my boxers.

Can you imagine what I would to you if I were there?

I want you to close your eyes and imagine I was

there right now, and you had just walked in after a long day of classes. You leave your bookbag by the door and kick the door shut with the back of your leg. Since your roommate is gone for the weekend, I've taken the liberty of airing out the room and lighting some candles, giving it a soft, ethereal glow.

You look amazing in the candlelight.

But you look even better when your tongue darts out to lick your dry lips.

As you walk toward me, you pause to kick off your shoes and push off your socks. You toss your socks into the hamper and leave your shoes by the door, giving me a generous view of your curvature, outlined by the thin fabric of your sweatpants. Then you bend down and slide them, leaving them in a heap on the floor.

When you spin around, I'm already sitting up and waiting for you.

You stop a few feet away from the bed and pull the hoodie up over your head, revealing a thin, see-through top underneath. Your nipples are already hard, and I can see their firm outline, making my fingers ache with impatience. Instead, I scooch closer to the edge of the bed and draw you toward me.

You make the most wonderful whimpering noise, Cara, and you melt against me, like it's the most natural thing in the world. When I tug on your hair, it comes undone, falling in waves around your shoulders and giving you a softer, more vulnerable look. As soon as you twist your arms behind you her head, my pulse quickens.

Can you see how hard you make me?

Can you hear how loud my breathing is?

I can hear how loud you are, how impatient and wet you are.

I know how much you want me, baby.

So I touch my lips to yours and nibble on your bottom lip.

You make a low, whimpering noise, and your lips part, allowing my tongue to dart in. As the two of us are kissing, I hoist you up and onto the bed. I pull back to look at you, and you're smiling up at me, eyes full of impatience and hunger. Fumbling in the dark, I grope around for the toy on the desk next to your bed.

Once my fingers close around it, my stomach tightens.

With a smile, I set it down on the mattress next to us and kiss you hard.

You taste like cherry flavored Coke.

It's my second favorite thing to taste.

Next to you.

I run my fingers up and down your arms, leaving a trail of heat in my wake, and you link your fingers over my neck. Then your legs come up around my waist, tightening. Without warning, I growl and rub myself against the inside of your leg. You're whimpering now, Cara, and I can sense how eager and impatient you are.

But we're not going to get ahead of ourselves.

There's still a lot of fun to be had, and I want to enjoy every inch of you.

And have you all to myself.

So I push you back down onto the mattress and pin your arms over your head. Using one hand, I keep your hands in place, and with the other, I pry your legs open. You're already wet, Cara, and the smell is making the blood in my veins turn molten. So I kneel down in between your legs and press my mouth to your center. I began to kiss you there, slowly at first, then I begin to make long, sweeping gestures that leave you panting and begging for more.

It's driving me crazy.

Just like you do.

Just like I want to do to you.

I release your arms and dig my nails into your waist, earning a hiss of pleasure as it passes through your lips. Slowly, I look up at you, and with your face framing your face and the look of impatience in your eyes, I know you feel it too, the electricity pulsing between us.

Do you feel like it's going to consume you whole?

Like it going to consume all of us?

Can you feel my dick moving inside of you, in between your wet folds?

Link your fingers over my neck, Cara.

There's a good girl.

Stop being so impatient. You and I have time. We have all weekend, in fact. So I squeeze my eyes shut and sweep my tongue back and forth. You thread your fingers through my hair and tighten your grip, sending a dual sensation of pain and pleasure ripping through me.

Do you have any idea how much I like that?

I bet you don't know.

Just like you don't know how sexy you are when you're in the throes of pleasure, giving yourself over to me completely. I know how insatiable and sexy you are, so I linger in between your legs, delaying your pleasure for as long as possible. Finally, you come with a violent shudder and call out my name.

Your body is slick with sweat when you look down at me.

I smirk at you, and your eyes turned hooded.

Abruptly, I crawl up to you and press my mouth to yours, letting you taste yourself there. You make a low, choked sound and bridge the distance between us. I feel your hand between us, but before it can dart lower, bringing our playtime to an end, I stop your progress. My hand circle your wrist, and I smile into the kiss.

I know you're confused, but I need you to trust me.

You need to know that if you touch me, it'll be over too quickly.

And I have no intention of letting that happen.

So I pin both arms over your head, holding them in a vise-like grip.

As you begin to squirm and wriggle, I pick up the vibrator and place it between us. It is cold and hard, and you immediately perk up at the sight of it. After I choose a low setting, I make sure you are comfortable, and I start using it.

You immediately go wild.

You are loud and impatient, and you keep reaching for me.

It takes every ounce of self-control I have to keep from removing the toy and thrusting into you myself. Once or twice, I even come close to doing it, when your fingers brush against me, and my cock twitches in response. Instead, I glance down at your face, your beautiful, tanned face, with a mole on the top right lip.

You know the one I love to kiss.

Your Marilyn Monroe mole.

You want to know a secret?

You're a lot sexier than she was.

Marilyn doesn't make me rock hard just by thinking of her. The sight of her twisting back and forth, like you are as you inch closer and closer to pleasure does nothing for me. One look at your face, and I release your hands and grip the sheets underneath us. Your hands fall to your sides, and you dig your nails into your palms. I can see how close you are, how turned on you are, but it still isn't enough.

I want you to beg for me, Cara.

You know how much I love to hear you beg, and you know how sexy it is when you do. This time, when you come again, you buck against the vibrator, twisting your head back and forth as you do. Eventually, you're covered in sweat and blindly groping for me in the darkness. I take your hands in mine, and I link them over my back.

I can feel how impatient you're getting and how badly you want me.

But it's not time yet.

Be patient, baby.

Because Daddy knows exactly what to do to make you scream with pleasure.

My hand falls between us, and I dart in between your wet folds. It isn't long before your juices coat my fingers and find your sweet spot. My finger moves inside of you, slow and steady until it's joined by another one. You grip my shoulders, throw your head back, and call out my name.

Fucking hell.

My name sounds like music on your lips.

Like the best fucking prayer in the world, and I can't get enough of it.

Using two fingers, I move inside of you, steadily at first then, when you begin to grind against me, I pump you harder. You are practically begging me now, and I have to press my lips together and brace myself, resisting every urge to bury myself inside of your sweet, tight little pussy.

But I know I will.

Once you're primed and begging for me to fuck you.

It is what you want, isn't it?

It's what you always want.

You spend all day hustling and working hard, so you can come home to me and be at my mercy. You love it when I take charge, Cara. I see the glint in your eyes when I do, and I can see it now as I finger-fuck you, pushing you closer and closer toward ecstasy. Finally, you come undone again, but this time you're quiet, your voice scarcely above a whisper. Your breathing is uneven when I kiss you, and you're breathless. Still, I feel you move against me, desperate for more.

Do you want to do know what I'd do next?

I'd stand up and bend you over, Cara.

I'd place one hand on either side of the bed, position myself behind you, and in one quick move, I'd be inside of you. You are panting harder and bucking against me, with wild and reckless abandon. But I move slowly, want to drag the moment out on even longer. I'm not ready to let it end, not ready to stop fucking you yet. So I dig my nails into your hips and ease in and out of you, using slow, steady thrusts.

I can feel your disappointment, Cara, and your impatience.

Because I know how hard and rough you like it.

I know you like it when I fuck your brains out and leave you weak in the knees.

Fuck, baby.

You must be so close, but I'm not done with you yet.

Instead, I flip you over, so you're on the edge of the bed, and I'm in between your legs. My eyes never leave your face as I throw your legs over my shoulders and thrust into you. Your muscles expand and contract around me, and I can smell your sexy, flowery perfume.

It's an intoxicating and heady mixture that I could drown in.

Your hands come up around my shoulders, and you shift.

I am balls deep inside of you, and it still isn't enough.

I want more.

So I bury my face in your neck and exhale.

You shudder when I spread your legs apart and sink deeper inside of you.

I want to stay in this moment with you, Cara.

You and I should keep fucking all night.

Before you come again, I ease out of you and pick you up. I set you down in front of your dorm room door and kick your legs apart. You place one hand on either side of the door and look back at me, and the look in your green eyes has me wondering.

It's never been this good for you, has it?

Since the moment you walked up to me at the real estate in company in your short skirt and a top that showed off your cleavage, I haven't been able to stop thinking of you. And when you pulled me into the bathroom later that day, and we fucked against the stalls, with my hand over your mouth, I knew then and there we had something special.

You're my special girl, Cara, and no one else can make you feel the way I do.

I don't want you to forget that while you're away at college, being ogled by all those other boys. None of them know you like I do. None of them can make you beg and writhe and pant like I do. Because I'm a man, and you need a real man who can pleasure you, who can bury himself inside of you for hours and bring you to the breaking point over and over again.

You twist your arms over your head and link them through my hair.

I make a low growling noise because of how good it feels, and the shivers that race up and down my spine when you do. Eventually, we are rocking back and forth against each other, the wooden door creaking against our weight. Then you turn around and jump up so your legs are wrapped around my waist.

Your small and tight little body fits against me as you press your lips to mine.

I kiss you soundly and thrust in and out of you.

You make low, little whimpering noises that echo through the thin walls.

Voices rise and fall outside, and I smirk, knowing your dormmates are jealous. I carry you against me and move back to the bed. Together, we fall backwards, and I catch a quick glimpse of delight on your face before I drape myself over you. You lift your legs up over your head, giving me better access. I reach between us and push your beasts together. Your nipples are rosy pink and hard.

I push your legs open, bend down, and take one nipple between my teeth.

Holy fuck.

I love how you taste, and it isn't long before I'm moving between both nipples, licking and sucking as if they were my lifeline. I feel you thread your fingers through my hair and pull. You are bucking and writhing against me, and my heart is pounding in my ears. With one last tug, I release your nipples and sit back. My eyes don't leave your face as I place a hand between us and stroke you.

You look up at me and smile.

Then you take my hand and move it closer to your center.

One finger darts in and another, and you're screaming again, this sound echoing off the walls and making my pulse quicken. I lean forward, and your legs are pinned against the headboard, leaving you squirming and writhing against me. You rake your fingers over my back, stop at my ass and squeeze.

You know what happens next, Daddy's special girl.

You and I come together, rocking back and forth against each other until we're spent. I stay inside of you until our breathing turns to normal. When I ease out of you, you pull me toward you, and we hold each other tight. You are absolutely satiated and spent and making low humming noises.

Fuck, I can't wait till your next visit.

Love,
    Daddy.

Afterword

Hey friends! It's Rayna again.

I really hope you enjoyed this new collection. If you did, I'd really appreciate a review. It only takes a minute, and it really helps people find my work. Leaving a review is a giant help!

And don't forget to check out my other anthologies. Just search "Rayna Russell" on Amazon or Audible.

And lastly, I welcome all your feedback. Drop me an email at RaynaRussellErotica@gmail.com

And if you want to submit a story, I'd love to read it! 3000 words is the sweet spot.

Thanks again for taking this ride with me. I hope you enjoyed the hell out of it!

XOXO,
    Rayna

www.ingramcontent.com/pod-product-compliance
Lightning Source LLC
Chambersburg PA
CBHW071921150726

47999CB00001B/64

9 798330 278541